In the domain of the Beast . . .

Candles lit themselves only a few feet ahead of me as I walked, and beyond them all was darkness; after I had passed, in a minute or two, they winked out again, as I saw when I turned once or twice to watch them. Looking up, I thought I saw a golden edge of light to a partly open door. My heart begin to beat very much faster.

Like all of the other doors I had met in the castle, this one opened at my approach. The room it revealed was a large, warm, and gracious one. On one wall to my left a fire was burning in a fireplace; two armchairs were drawn up before it. One chair was empty. In the other a massive shadow sat. I caught a gleam of dark-green velvet on what might have been a knee in the shadowed armchair.

"Good evening, Beauty," said a great harsh voice. "I am the Beast."

BOOKS BY
ROBIN MCKINLEY

ROBIN McKINLEY

BEAUTY

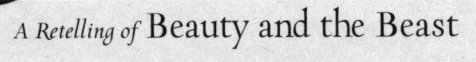

A *Retelling of* Beauty and the Beast

 GREENWILLOW BOOKS,

AN IMPRINT OF HarperCollins Publishers

Beauty:

A Retelling of Beauty and the Beast

Text copyright © 1978, 2018 by Robin McKinley

Illustrations copyright © 2018 by Diana Sudyka

First Greenwillow paperback edition, 2018

Library of Congress Cataloging-in-Publication Data

McKinley, Robin.

Beauty : a retelling of Beauty and the beast

ISBN 978-0-06-280345-0 (pbk.)

[1. Fairy tales. 2. Folklore.] I. Beauty and the beast. II. Title.

PZ8.M1793Be 813'.5'4 [398.2] 77-25636

18 19 20 21 22 CG/BRR 10 9 8 7 6 5 4 3 2 1

Greenwillow Books

To my mother,

because it will be a long wait for Kilkerran;

and to both Mr. Rochesters,

for aiding Mahomet to go to the mountain.

Part One

I was the youngest of three daughters. Our literal-minded mother named us Grace, Hope, and Honour, but few people except perhaps the minister who had baptized all three of us remembered my given name. My father still likes to tell the story of how I acquired my odd nickname: I had come to him for further information when I first discovered that our names meant something besides you-come-here. He succeeded in explaining grace and hope, but he had some difficulty trying to make the concept of honour understandable to a five-year-old. I heard him out, but with an expression of deepening disgust; and when he was finished I said: "Huh! I'd rather be Beauty."

He laughed; and over the next few weeks told everyone he met this story of his youngest child's precocity. I found that my ill-considered opinion became a reality; the name at least was attached to me securely.

All three of us were pretty children, with curly blond hair and blue-grey eyes; and if Grace's hair was the brightest, and Hope's eyes the biggest, well, for the first ten years the difference wasn't too noticeable. Grace, who was seven years older than I, grew into a beautiful, and profoundly graceful, young girl. Her hair was wavy and fine and luxuriant, and as butter-yellow as it had been when she was a baby (said doting friends of the family), and her eyes were long-lashed and as blue as a clear May morning after rain (said her doting swains). Hope's hair darkened to a rich chestnut-brown, and her big eyes turned a smoky green. Grace was an inch or two the taller, and her skin was rosy where Hope's was ivorypale; but except for their dramatic coloring my sisters looked very much alike. Both were tall and slim, with tiny waists, short straight noses, dimples when they smiled, and small delicate hands and feet.

I was five years younger than Hope, and I don't know what happened to me. As I grew older, my hair turned mousy, neither blond nor brown, and the baby curl fell out until all that was left was a stubborn refusal to co-operate with the curling iron; my eyes turned a muddy hazel. Worse, I didn't grow; I was thin, awkward, and undersized, with big long-fingered hands and huge feet. Worst of all, when I turned thirteen, my skin broke out in spots. There hadn't been a spot in our mother's family for centuries, I was sure. And Grace and Hope went on being innocently and ravishingly lovely, with every eligible young man—and many more that were neither—dying of love for them.

Since I was the baby of the family I was a little spoiled. Our mother died less than two years after I was born, and our little sister Mercy died two weeks after her. Although we had a series of highly competent and often affectionate nursemaids and governesses, my sisters felt that they had raised me. By the time it was evident that I was going to let the family down by being plain, I'd been called Beauty for over six years; and while I came to hate the name, I was too proud to ask that it be discarded. I wasn't really very fond of my given name, Honour, either, if it came to that: It sounded sallow and angular to me, as if "honourable" were the best that could be said of me. My sisters were too kind to refer to the increasing inappropriateness of my nickname. It was all the worse that they were as good-hearted as they were beautiful, and their kindness was sincerely meant.

Our father, bless him, didn't seem to notice that there was any egregious, and deplorable, difference between his first two daughters and his youngest. On the contrary, he used to smile at us over the dinner table and say how pleased he was that we were growing into three such dissimilar individuals; that he always felt sorry for families who looked like petals from the same flower. For a while his lack of perception hurt me, and I suspected him of hypocrisy; but in time I came to be grateful for his generous blindness. I could talk to him openly, about my dreams for the future, without fear of his pitying me or doubting my motives.

The only comfort I had in being my sisters' sister was that I was "the clever one." To a certain extent this was damning me with faint praise, in the same category as accepting my given name as an epithet accurately reflecting my limited worth—it was the best that could be said of me. Our governesses had always remarked on my cleverness in a pitying tone of voice. But at least it was true. My intellectual abilities gave me a release, and an excuse. I shunned company because I preferred books; and the dreams I confided to my father were of becoming a scholar in good earnest, and going to University. It was unheard of that a woman should do anything of the sort—as several shocked governesses were only too quick to tell me, when I spoke a little too boldly—but my father nodded and smiled and said, "We'll see." Since I believed my father could do anything—except of course make me pretty—I worked and studied with passionate dedication, lived in hope, and avoided society and mirrors.

Our father was a merchant, one of the wealthiest in the city. He was the son of a shipwright, and had gone to sea as a cabin boy when he was not yet ten years old; but by the time he was forty, he and his ships were known in most of the major ports of the world. When he was forty, too, he married our mother, the Lady Marguerite, who was just seventeen. She came of a fine old family that had nothing but its bloodlines left to live on, and her parents were more than happy to accept my father's suit, with its generous bridal settlements. But it had been a happy marriage, old friends told us girls. Our father had doted on his lovely young wife—my two sisters took after her, of course, except that her hair had been red-gold and her eyes amber—and she had worshiped him.

When I was twelve, and Grace was nineteen, she became engaged to our father's most promising young captain, Robert Tucker, a blue-eyed, black-haired giant of twenty-eight. He set sail almost immediately after their betrothal was announced, on a voyage that was to take three long years but bode fair to make his fortune. There had been a Masque of Courtesy acted out among the three of them—Robbie, Grace, and Father—when the plans for the voyage and the wedding had first been discussed. Father suggested that they should be married right away, that they might have a few weeks together (and perhaps start a baby, to give Grace something to do while she waited the long months for his return) before he set sail. The journey could be delayed a little.

Nay, said Robbie, he wished to prove himself first; it was no man's trick to leave his wife in her father's house; if he could not care for her himself as she deserved, then he was no fit husband for her. But he could not yet afford a house of his own, and three years was a long time; perhaps she should be freed of the constraints of their betrothal. It was not fair to one so fair as she to be asked to wait so long. And then of course Grace in her turn stood up and said that she would wait twenty years if necessary, and it would be the greatest honour of her life to have the banns published immediately. And so they were; and Robbie departed a month later.

Grace told Hope and me at great length about this Masque, just after it happened. We sat over tea in Grace's rose silk hung sitting room. Her tea service was very fine, and she presided over the silver urn like a grand and gracious hostess, handing round her favorite cups to her beloved sisters as if we too were grand ladies. I put mine down hastily; after years of taking tea with my sisters, I still eyed the little porcelain cups askance, and preferred to wait until I could return to my study and ring for my maid to bring me a proper big mug of tea, and some biscuits.

Hope looked vague and dreamy; I was the only one who saw any humour in Grace's story—although I could appreciate that it had not been amusing for the principals—but then, I was the only one who read poetry for pleasure. Grace blushed when she mentioned the baby, and admitted that while Robbie was right, of course, she was a weak woman and wished—oh, just the littlest bit!—that they might have been married before he left. She was even more beautiful when she blushed. Her sitting room set her high color off admirably.

Those first months after Robbie set sail must have been very long ones for her. She who had been the toast of the town now went to parties very seldom; when Hope and Father protested that there was no need of her living like a nun; she smiled seraphically and said she truly didn't wish to go out and mix with a great many people anymore. She spent most of her time "setting her linen in order" as she put it; she sewed very prettily—I don't believe she had set a crooked stitch since she hemmed her first sheet at the age of five—and she already had a trousseau that might have been the envy of any three girls.

So Hope went out alone, with our chaperone, the last of our outgrown governesses, or sponsored by one of the many elderly ladies who thought she was just delightful. But after two years or so, it was observed that the incomparable Hope also began to neglect many fashionable gatherings; an incomprehensible development, since no banns had been published and no mysterious wasting diseases were whispered about. It was made comprehensible to me one night when she crept into my bedroom, weeping.

I was up late, translating Sophocles. She explained to me that she had to tell someone, but she couldn't be so selfish as to bother Grace when she was preoccupied with Robbie's safety—"Yes, I understand," I said patiently, although I privately thought Grace would be the better for the distraction of someone else's problems—but she, Hope, had fallen in love with Gervain Woodhouse, and was therefore miserable. I sorted out this curious statement eventually.

Gervain was an estimable young man in every way—but he was also an ironworker in Father's shipyard. His family were good and honest people, but not at all grand, and his prospects were no more than modest. He had some ideas about the ballasting of ships, which Father admired, and had been invited to the house several times to discuss them, and then stayed on to tea or supper. I supposed that this was how he and my sister had met. I didn't follow Hope's account of their subsequent romance very well, and didn't at all recognize her anguished lover as the reserved and polite young man that Father entertained. At any rate, Hope concluded, she knew Father expected her to make a great match, or at least a good one, but her heart was given.

"Don't be silly," I told her. "Father only wants you to be happy. He's delighted with the prospect of Robbie as a son-in-law, you know, and Grace might have had an earl."

Hope's dimples showed. "An elderly earl."

"An earl is an earl," I said severely. "Better than your count, who turned out to have a wife in the attic. If you think you'll be happiest scrubbing tar out of burlap aprons,

Father won't say nay. And," I added thoughtfully, "he will probably buy you several maids to do the scrubbing."

Hope sighed. "You are not the slightest bit romantic."

"You knew that already," I said. "But I *do* remind you that Father is not an ogre, as you know very well if you'd only calm down and think about it. He himself started as a shipwright; and you know that still tells against us in some circles. Only Mother was real society. Father hasn't forgotten. And he likes Gervain."

"Oh, Beauty," Hope said; "but that's not all. Ger only stays in the city for love of me; he doesn't really like it here, nor ships and the sea. He was born and raised north of here, far inland. He misses the forests. He wants to go back, and be a blacksmith again."

I thought about this. It seemed like the waste of a first-class ironworker. I was also, for all my scholarship, not entirely free of the city bred belief that the north was a land rather overpopulated by goblins and magicians, who went striding about the countryside muttering wild charms. In the city magic was more discreetly contained, in little old men and women with bright eyes, who made up love potions and cures for warts in return for modest sums. But if this didn't bother Hope, there was no reason it should bother me.

I said at last: "Well, we'll miss you. I hope you won't settle too far away—but it's still not an insurmountable obstacle. Look here: Stop wringing your hands and listen to me. Would you like me to talk to Father about it first, since you're so timid?"

"Oh, that would be wonderful of you," my brighteyed sister said eagerly. "I've made Gervain promise not to say anything yet, and he feels that our continued silence is not right." It was a tradition in the family that I could "get around" Father best: I was the baby, and so on. This was another of my sisters' tactful attempts at recompense for the way I looked, but there was some truth to it. Father would do anything for any of us, but my sisters were both a little in awe of him.

"Umm, yes," I said, looking longingly at my books. "I'll talk to Father—but give me a week or so, will you please, since you've waited this long. Father's got business troubles, as you may have noticed, and I'd like to pick my time."

Hope nodded, cheerful again, called me a darling girl, kissed me, and slipped out of the room. I went back to Sophocles. But to my surprise, I couldn't concentrate; stories I'd heard of the northland crept in and disrupted the Greek choruses. And there was also the fact that Ger, safe and sensible Ger, found our local witches amusing; it was not that he laughed when they were mentioned, but that he became very still. In my role of tiresome little sister, I had harassed him about this, till he told me a little. "Where I come from, any old wife can mix a poultice to take off warts; it's something she learns from her mother with how to hem a shirt and how to make gingerbread. Or if she can't, she certainly has a neighbor who can, just as her husband probably has a good useful spell or two to stuff into his scarecrow with the straw, to make it do its work a little better." He saw that he had his audience's fixed attention, so he grinned at me, and added: "There are even a few dragons left up north, you know. I saw one once, when I was a boy, but they don't come that far south very often." Even I knew that dragons could do all sorts of marvelous things, although only a great magician could master one.

My opportunity to discuss Hope's future with Father never arrived. The crash came only a few days after my sister's and my midnight conversation. The little fleet of merchant ships Father owned had hit a streak of bad luck; indeed, since Robert Tucker had set sail in the *White Raven* three years ago, with the *Windfleet*, the *Stalwart*, and the *Fortune's Chance* to bear her company, nothing had gone right. Shipments were canceled, crops were poor, revolutions disturbed regular commerce; Father's ships were sunk in storms, or captured by pirates; many of his warehouses were destroyed, and the clerks disappeared or returned home penniless.

The final blow was a message brought by a weary, footsore man who had set sail as third mate on the *Stalwart* three years ago. The four ships had been driven apart by a sudden storm. The *Stalwart* and the *Windfleet* had been driven up on the shore and destroyed; only a handful of men survived. The *Fortune's Chance* was later discovered to have been taken by pirates who found it lost and disabled after the storm. Of the *White Raven* there was no word, of ship or crew, but it was presumed lost. The captain of the *Windfleet* had survived the wreck of the two ships, but at the cost of a crushed leg that refused to heal. A year ago the sailor who stood now, shredding his hat with his hands, had been sent by that captain with one other man, to try and work their way home and deliver their messages, and an urgent plea for assistance, since written letters seemed to have gone astray. There had been a dozen men left alive when the pair had set out, but their situation, alone in a strange country, was precarious.

The sailor's companion had died by foul play, and he had heard nothing of the men he had left since shortly after his departure.

I don't remember the next few weeks, after the sailor's arrival, too well; nor do I regret that vagueness. I remember only too clearly that Father, who had been young and hearty, in a few days' time came to look his age, which was past sixty; and poor Grace turned as white as cold wax when she heard the news, and went about the house like a silent nightmare, like the poor pale girls in old ballads who fade away until they are nothing more than grey omens to the living. Hope and I took turns trying to persuade our father and eldest sister to eat, and making sure that the fires in their rooms were well built up.

Father made plans to take what little remained to him and us and retire to the country, where we could make shift to live cheaply. His rapid rise in business wealth and success had been based on his ability to take calculated risks. He had run ventures very near to the line before, and always come about, and so he had refused to believe that he would not come about at the last moment this time too. Consequently, our ruin was complete, for he had kept nothing in reserve. What little he had available to him he used to try and cushion the fall for some of his best men; most of it was sent with the third mate from the *Stalwart*, to try and find the men he had left behind him and help them out of their difficulties. The man left on his return journey less than a week after his arrival, although Father urged him to stay and rest, and send someone else in his stead. But he was anxious to see himself how his fellow crew members fared, and he would have the best chance of finding them again; he did not say it, but we knew that he was also anxious to leave the sight of us and the ruin he had brought to us, although it was none of his creation or blame.

The house and lands were to be auctioned off; the money resulting would enable us to start again. But start what? Father was a broken man; he was now also labeled jinxed, and no other merchant would have anything to do with him, if he could have brought himself to work for another man. He had done no carpentry but trinkets for his daughters since he had given up shipbuilding for more lucrative business over thirty years ago; and he had no other marketable skills.

It was at this low ebb in our thoughts and plans that Gervain came to visit us; this was about a week after the man from the *Stalwart* had told his story. The four of us were sitting silent in the parlour after dinner; usually we talked, or Father or myself read aloud while my sisters sewed, but we had little heart for such amusements now. The auction had already been set, for a day late next week; and Father had begun looking for a little house somewhere far from the city.

Gervain was announced. Hope blushed scarlet, and then looked down quickly at her clasped hands. She had told me two days before that she had refused to see Gervain since the news of our downfall had come. There was no question of his not knowing; the whole city was talking about it. Father's shipyard was being sold first of all to pay off business debts, and all the employees were wondering what their new master would be like, and if they would even still have jobs. Father had been both liked and respected by the men who worked for him— and admired for his daring in business ventures.

Gervain explained the reason for his visit without preamble. He had looked forward, a few weeks ago, to making an offer, soon, for Hope's hand. He understood that everything was suddenly changed; but he thought that he knew his own heart, and dared to trust that he knew Hope's. When he had first wished to marry Hope and she had given him to believe that she would be willing to leave the city for a humbler life if her family consented, he had begun to look for an opening suitable to his skills as a blacksmith, through friends he still had living in the town of his childhood. He had heard just this afternoon of a house, with a shop and a forge and work waiting, in a small town only a few miles from the village he had been born and raised in.

His suggestion was this: that he would be honoured if we would throw our fortune in with his. The house would be a bit small for five, but it could be enlarged; and, he added with a bow to Father, there was a bit of a carpenter's shed with the blacksmith's shop, and work for a good craftsman. He would not press his suit now, and we were not to think that any obligation fell on Hope to marry him as a reward for any trifling service such as he might be able to render us. He was sure that while such service might now seem more than might honourably be accepted, he knew that we only needed an introduction to a new way of life for us to make our own way, with honour. He would be deeply grateful to us if we allowed him to make that introduction.

Father sat silent for a long moment after Gervain had done. Ger had been offered a seat when he first entered, and had refused it, now he stood as calmly as if he were in his own home waiting for dinner to be served. He was a good-looking man, though no beauty, with brown hair and serious grey eyes; I put his age at around thirty. He had worked for Father about six years, and was proved a steady and honest craftsman.

Father said at last: "Hope, what this young man has said of you is true?" and Hope, blushing and paling by turns like an autumn sunset seen through wind-shaken leaves, nodded and said, "Yes, Father." He raised his head then and looked at Ger, who had not moved but to breathe and follow our father with his eyes. "Gervain, I do not know if I do the right thing in my reply, for it is a heavy task you ask the burden of, for all your pretty words. But indeed I and my daughters are in sore need of help." He looked round at us. "And we will, I think, be most grateful to accept what you offer."

Gervain bowed his head. "Thank you, Mr. Huston. I will, if I may, call on you sometime tomorrow, that we may discuss arrangements."

"Anytime that is convenient for you," said Father, and with a touch of grim humour, added, "You may be sure of finding me here."

I don't know what we would have done without Gervain. Since we had first known that the worst had happened, our lives had seemed to come to a halt: We could see no farther than each bleak day's dawning, and the thought of the auction and the end of the life we had known seemed the end of life itself. We drifted through the hours like abandoned ships on a sea without horizon. Gervain's plans, which, after a long afternoon's conversation with our father, he was careful to explain to all of us, gave us something to think about. He was patient with everything but gloomy forebodings; encouraged questions, told us stories about the hilly, forested land we were going to that he loved so well; and, by his quiet enthusiasm, struck answering sparks of interest in our tired hearts. We had known that we would leave the city and travel, probably far away and out of reach of old friends and associations. Now we knew that we were bound for a little four-room house in a town called Blue Hill, with the deep hills on one side and forests at front and back, and that our journey there was likely to take between six weeks and two months. We even began to take some interest in the practical aspects of the trip as Gervain described horses and wagons and roads.

It was easiest for Hope and me. I was the youngest, I was in love with no one except perhaps Euripides, and while I grieved deeply for my father and for Grace, there was little in the city or our life there that I loved for itself—

although rather more that I took for granted, like my own maid and all the books that I wanted. I was frightened of the unknown that we faced, and of our ignorance; but I had never been afraid of hard work, I had no beauty to lose, nor would there be any wrench at parting from high society. I didn't relish the thought of sleeping in an attic and washing my own clothes, but then it didn't fill me with horror either, and I was still young enough to see it in the light of an adventure.

Hope had told me weeks before that Gervain's original plans had included a maid to do the heavy work, and four rooms would have been sufficient if not ample for the two of them (our house in town had eighteen rooms, including a ballroom two stories tall, plus kitchens and servants' quarters). These latter days she was subdued, but there was an air of suppressed excitement about her. Once started on a task that could be finished in one effort, she would accomplish it efficiently enough; but she was absentminded about messages, or about remembering to return to a task only partially completed. She confessed to me one night that she felt guilty for feeling so happy: It was very selfish of her to be glad that she was going with Gervain, yet would not be moving away from her family.

"Don't be silly," I said. "Seeing your happiness is

what's holding the other two together." Nearly every night, after Grace and Father had gone to bed, Hope and I met, usually in my bedroom, to discuss how "the other two" were doing, and whether there was anything further that might be done for them. And for Hope to ease the tension of being quiet during the day for her father's and elder sister's sakes by babbling at length to me about how wonderful Gervain was. "Besides," I added after a moment, "washing your own floors will be enough and plenty of reality for you."

"Don't forget the tarry aprons you prophesied before," Hope said, smiling.

No one mentioned goblins or dragons or magicians.

2

The day of the auction came all too soon. The three of us spent it locked up in Grace's sitting room, which had been reserved from the sale proceedings for the use of the family, shivering in each other's arms, and listening to the strange voices and strange footsteps walking in our rooms. Gervain was in charge; Father had been bundled off to spend the day going over records at the shipyard; it was Ger who had the lists of items to be sold and saved, and it was he who answered questions.

At the end of the day, Ger knocked on our door and said gently, "It's all over; come out now, and have some tea." Much of the furniture was left, for we had been left the house and "fittings" for the two more weeks Ger had estimated it would take us to be packed up finally and gone. But many of the small pieces—Father's Chinese bowl, the smaller Oriental rugs, vases, little tables, the paintings off the walls—were gone, and the house looked forlorn. The three of us wandered from room to room clinging to each other's hands, and silently counting the missing articles in the last sad rays of the setting sun. The house smelled of tobacco smoke and strange perfumes.

Ger, after leaving us half an hour alone, swept us up from the drawing room where we had collapsed at last—it had suffered the fewest depredations of any of the rooms—and said, "Come downstairs, see what your friends have left you," and refusing to say more, ushered us down to the kitchen. Father met us on the front stair, gazing at a dark rectangular spot in the wallpaper, and was brought along. Downstairs, on tables and chairs and in the pantry were laid haphazard any number of things, much of it food: smoked hams and bacon and venison, sealed jars of vegetables and preserves, and a few precious ones of apples and peaches and apricots. There were bolts of cloth, gingham and chintz, muslin, linen, and fine-woven wool; there were leathers, soft and supple and carefully stretched; and there were three heavy fur capes. There was also a canary in a cage, who tried a trill on us when we peered in at him.

"You should not have let them do this," said Father.

"Indeed, I did not know," Ger said, "and I am glad I did not, for I am not sure I would have tried to stop anyone. But I only discovered it myself a few minutes ago."

Father stood frowning; he had been very firm in resisting offers of charity, and in paying all his debts, even when fellow merchants were willing to cancel them silently, for old friendship's sake.

A few servants had pleaded to stay with us, even without pay, until we left; and although we could ill afford even to feed them, Father could not quite bring himself to send them away. One of them, a young woman named Ruth, came down the scullery stairs now and said, "Excuse me, Mr. Huston; there's a man here to see Miss Beauty."

"All right," I said, wondering who it might be. "You might as well send him down here." Father made a restless motion, but said nothing. The rest of us looked at one another for a moment, and then there was the tread of heavy boots on the stairs, and Tom Black appeared in the doorway.

Tom bred, raised, and trained horses; he had a

stable in the city, and a stud farm outside the city, and an excellent reputation throughout a large portion of the country. He sold hacks and hunters and carriage horses for his livelihood; all our animals had come from him. My sisters had owned, up until this morning, two pretty, round little mares with gentle manners; and for me, who looked slightly better in the saddle than anywhere else, there had been a long lean chestnut gelding who could jump over anything that stayed in one place long enough for him to gallop up to it. But Tom's real love was for the Great Horses, eighteen hands high and taller, descended from the big, heavy horses the knights had used to carry themselves and several hundred pounds of armour into battle at an earth-breaking gallop. Many draft horses pulling carts and ploughs across the country owed their size and strength to the diluted blood of these old chargers; but the horses Tom bred were sleek and beautiful, and ridden by princes.

"Your horse," he said to me. "I've left him in the stable for you. Thought I'd best tell you, so you could go down, say hello, settle him in; he'll get lonesome by himself, now that all the little stuff is gone." The little stuff was our riding and carriage horses, which had been taken away by their new owners. "And his saddle. It's only an old one. A bit worn. But it'll do you for a bit."

I was looking at him blankly.

"Don't gape at me, girl," said Tom irritably. "Greatheart. He's in the stable, waiting for you. I'm telling you to go say good night to him or he won't sleep for worrying."

"You can't give me Greatheart," I said at last.

"I'm not giving him to you," replied Tom. "There's no giving about it. He's won't eat if you go off without him. I know it. He's already been missing you these last weeks; you come around so rarely, it makes him uneasy. So you take him with you. He's a big strong horse. You'll find uses for him."

"But—Tom," I said desperately, wondering why no one else was saying anything. "He's a tremendously valuable horse—you can't want one of your Great Horses pulling a cart, which is all there'll be for him with us. He should carry the King."

"He wouldn't like carrying the King," said Tom. "He'll do what you tell him to. I didn't think I had to tell you to be good to him, but I'm wishing you'd stop talking nonsense to me and go down to the stable. He'll be worrying that you don't come. Night, miss," he said, nodding to each of the three of us, "sir," to Father and

Gervain. And he stamped back up the stairs again.

We heard Ruth let him out; silence came to us on the backwash of the front door closing. "I guess I'd better go do what he says," I said vaguely, still staring at the empty stairs. Father started to laugh: the first real laugh we'd heard from him since the trouble began. "They're all too much for us," he said. "Bless them, we'd best leave town soon before we have too much to carry away."

"What is this horse that won't eat if you leave it be hind?" inquired Gervain.

I shook my head. "That's all rubbish—he's just giving him to me. I don't know why. I used to lurk around his stable a lot."

"Horses are the only things that will take her away from her precious Greek poets," said Hope. "And Tom says she's the only woman he knows who can ride properly."

I ignored her. "One of Tom's mares died giving birth, he said the foal might have a chance if someone who had the time and patience would bottle-feed it. So I did. I named the poor thing Greatheart—well, I was only eleven. That was four years ago. Tom usually sells them when they're four or five. He let me do some of the training—not just the basic breaking to saddle; all his

Great Horses learn some fancy steps, and how to behave on parade, how to stand at attention. Well I guess I'd better go."

"She used to read him her Greek translations," murmured Grace. "And he survived."

"It gave her governess *fits*," said Hope. "But then I'm sure that horse knows more Greek than Miss Stanley did."

I glowered at her. "He was here for a while, then I took him back to Tom's stable when he was a yearling—but I've visited him nearly every day—except, uh, recently." I started up the stairs. "I'll be back in a little. Don't eat all the biscuits; I still want my tea."

"Can I come along and meet your horse?" said Ger.

"Of course," I said.

Twelve days after the auction I rode Greatheart, with Grace riding pillion, out of the city we'd lived in all our lives, for the last time. The rest of the family rode in the long wooden wagon we followed. Ger was driving, and Hope sat beside him, with her arm around Father, who sat on the outside. None of us looked back. We were traveling with a group of wagoners who made this journey regularly twice a year: It began in the broad farm country south of the city and wound its way from town to town to the far north; they arrived at their final destination with only a few weeks to spare before they turned back and went south again. These men knew the road and what dangers it might offer, and were always willing—for a reasonable fee—to have a few pilgrims journey with them. Conveniently for us, the train passed about ten miles from the village that was to be our new home. Hope and I agreed, during one of our late-evening conversations, that this made us feel a little less desolate, a little less cut off from the rest of humanity and the world.

I remembered, from several years ago, a family we had known a little whose fortunes in the city had suddenly collapsed; they had left in these same wagons with this same group. It had never occurred to me then to consider the possibility that we might one day follow them.

Greatheart clopped along, nearly asleep, chewing meditatively on his bits; one of his easy strides reached as far as two of the small, sturdy wagon horses'. There had been a little difficulty about bringing him at all, for a riding horse was an expensive luxury; he was also a very visible incentive to any bold thief who might be watching us. But spring was well advanced, so there was no shortage of fresh fodder for my massive horse's matching appetite, and I promised to break him to harness as soon as we were moved into our new home. Gervain shook his head over us, but I don't think he ever meant to suggest that Greatheart be left behind. The wagoners shook their heads too, and muttered loudly that they who could afford to own a horse like that one could afford to travel in a party of their own, with hired guards, and not disturb their humble company with flashy lures to robbers and cutthroats. But the train was doing some business for Tom Black's stable too, and the story must have come out, for several of the wagoners came up to us during the first few days to look at Greatheart a little more carefully, and with a little more sympathy—and curiosity.

One of them said to me: "And so this is the horse that wouldn't eat if you left him behind, eh, missy?" and slapped the horse's neck jovially. His name was Tom, also, Tom Bradley; and he began to come to our campfire in the evenings sometimes as the days of the journey mellowed into weeks and we all grew more accustomed to one another. Most of the wagoners kept to themselves; they had seen too many travelers in reduced circumstances going to new, unknown homes and destinies to be particularly interested in them. They ignored us, not unkindly but with indifference, as they ignored almost everything but the arrangement of harness and the stacking of loads, the condition of the horses and wagons, the roads, and the weather. Tom Bradley's visits were very welcome to us, then, because even with Gervain's ready cheerfulness and optimism we were all inclined to gloom. None of us was accustomed to long, bruising hours either on horseback—which was preferable—or in the wagon, which was built to carry heavy loads, and not sprung or cushioned for tender human freight.

"Eh, now," Tom would say; "you're doing none so bad; and it'll get better in a week or two, as you get used to the way of it. Have a bit of stew, now, you'll feel good as new." Tom knew all there was to know about cooking in a single pot over a small fire, and taught us how to bury potatoes in the embers. And when Grace's saddle sores grew so painful that she could get no sleep at night, he mysteriously found her a sheepskin to sit on, and would take no payment for it. "They call me the nurse-maid," he said with a grin, "the rest of 'em do; but I don't mind it. Somebody has to look out for you innocents—if nobody did there'd be trouble soon because you've no proper notion how to take care of yourselves. Excepting of course you, sir," he said with a nod to Ger, who gave a short laugh.

"I'm no less grateful for your help than the others,

Tom," he said. "I know little about wagons, as you've found out by now."

Tom chuckled. "Ah, well, I've been twenty—nearer thirty—years at this, and there's little I don't know about wagons, or shouldn't be, for shame. I've no family I go home to, you see, so I take to whoever needs me on these journeys. And I'll say this to you now, as I'll say it again when you leave us to go your way. I'm wishing you the best of good luck, and I don't say that often. Nurse-maiding is a mixed blessing, more often than not. But I'll be sorry to see the last of you folks."

The journey lasted two long months, and by the time we parted company with the wagoners we were all covered with saddle sores, lame and aching in every inch of bone, muscle, and skin, from sleeping on the ground, and heartily sick of the whole business. The only ones relatively unaffected by what seemed to us girls to be desperate hardship were Gervain and Greatheart; Ger was still as certain and cheerful as he had been ever since he first entered our town parlour over three months ago, and Greatheart still strode amiably along at the tail of the train as if he hadn't a care in the world. We were all thinner, harder, and shaggier. Tom shook hands all around, and tickled Greatheart under his whiskery chin;

wished us good luck as he had promised; and said that he'd see us in about six months. He would be coming to say hello, and to collect the wagon and pair of horses we were taking with us now.

The unaccustomed rigours of travel had deadened us to much looking around at the countryside we passed. Mostly we noticed the ruts in the road, the rocks under our blankets, and the way the leaves on the trees we chose to lie under always dripped dew. As we turned off the main road towards our new home, now only a few miles away, we looked around with the first real interest we had felt for the land we were traveling over.

We were well inland now, far from any sight or smell of the sea; and it was a hilly country, unlike the low-lying and many-rivered area we had left. We parted from our companions of the road at dawn, and in the late afternoon we found ourselves on the main, and only, street of Blue Hill. Children had cried a warning of our approach, and men had looked up, shading their eyes to stare across their small, hilly, carefully cut and tilled fields. We saw young wheat growing, and corn, oats, and barley; there were cattle and sheep and pigs and goats, and a few sturdy, shaggy horses in harness. Most of the men went back to their work; newcomers would keep, but the daylight wouldn't; but in town there were a dozen or more people collected and waiting to welcome us, and to look us over.

Ger, wizard-like, produced an aunt with six children, who ran the tiny public house; it was she who had heard that he wanted to bring a new bride back to the hills he'd grown up in, and had written him about the empty smithy in her home town. Her smile made us, waifs in the wilderness, feel that perhaps we weren't utterly lost and forsaken after all. She introduced us to the other people who were standing around, several of whom recognized Ger, or pretended to, as the young lad from over the next hill who'd gone south to the city over ten years ago. Ger's birthplace and childhood home, Goose Landing, named for the fine winter hunting, and our new home, Blue Hill, had no particular boundaries beyond the little main streets; the farms and fields spread themselves disinterestedly between the Sign of the Dancing Cat, in Goose Landing, and the Red Griffin, Ger's aunt's establishment.

Ger's aunt's name was Melinda Honeybourne, and she was a widow of four years, having taken over the entire management of the Griffin, which they had owned together, after her husband's death. She told the two eldest children, who were standing bashfully at the

Griffin's front gate, to look after it and the younger ones, while she climbed into our wagon and came with us "to see our new house." I picked up the two smallest children and put them in front of me in Greatheart's saddle.

The house was located beyond the edge of town and isolated from it by the eyeless backs of the village houses, by a few stands of trees left at this far end of town where they were in nobody's way yet, and by the gentle undulations of the land. Most of the farms lay east of the village in an irregular patchwork of forest and field and stream, on both sides of the main road. Goose Landing lay mostly out of sight beyond the big forested hill to the southwest, with farmlands creeping round its feet and clasping hands at its skirts. The nearest town to the north was Sunnyfield, a three days' journey, perhaps, through the heavy forest to Blue Hill's northwest, but no one ever went that way, and it was at least a week's journey to go around it. Our house's back was to this great wood that no one passed through.

"Although I've no call to say I've come to see it, for see it I have many times. Since I could not be certain when you'd finally be coming I've been going up once a week, twice when I could manage it, or sending one of the older ones, to open the windows and let some fresh air inside. A closed-up house stales overnight, or nearly, and that's no proper welcome." Melinda addressed herself to Grace, who was riding in the wagon. "You'll find it clean enough to move into, miss, though of course you'll be wanting to scrub it yourself once you've settled. But it's been boarded up and empty for two years, and the dust was sticky-thick on everything, so Molly—she's my eldest—and me, we washed everything right well, three months ago, when we heard you were coming for sure. Moving's a sorry business at best, and it'd make things a bit more comfortable for you. Mind you, though, you're welcome at the Griffin till you're fixed up the way you like. I'm used to sudden company for bed and board, and I like it."

Grace began to thank her for her trouble, but she brushed it away, saying kindly, "And you needn't worry that you owe us anything, for be sure I'll take it out of young Ger here when he gets the shop going again. Ah, we're all delighted to be having our own smith again; it's a long way from this side of the hill to the Goose forge, you know, and we're not all of us too pleased with young Henney's skill besides. You've not forgotten the right ways of doing things, there in that city, now, have you, Ger?"

"No indeed: I'm still as clever as the devil himself," Ger said, and Melinda laughed; but he'd seen Father wince when she, noticing nothing, had spoken with a countrywoman's scorn of towns.

The two babies I had collected were named Daphne and Rachel; Daphne was the elder, and would answer direct questions after a long pause spent considering the inquirer's motives. Rachel said nothing at all, and held on to Greatheart's mane with both hands. Both of them seemed delighted to be sitting six feet above the ground and not at all frightened, although somewhat annoyed at my desire for conversation.

"There it is," said Melinda.

The street had faded to a track, which then led vaguely over a small rise in the ground, and there in a shallow dish of a meadow stood a little weather-brown wooden house with a shed beside it, and a smaller shed built out from the larger one. At first sight the house seemed as tiny as a doll's, delicately carved out of matchsticks, till I realized that this was the effect of the great forest that began only a few hundred feet behind it, with saplings and scrub growing up nearly to its back door. There had once been a fence around a kitchen garden in the back, but it was a jungle of vines and great leafy things gone to seed. A third shed hidden behind the other two we discovered to be a stable, with only two narrow stalls and a leaky roof. There was a well on the small hill we'd come over following the road from the town, but a lovely bright stream jingled its way down from the forest and took a generous bend to be convenient to the forge before it disappeared behind another small hill, heading away from the town.

We had all been dreading this final moment of finding out just what we had come to, and we all took heart at the quiet scene before us. The late-afternoon sun gilded the early-summer green of the meadow, and stained the pink and white daisies to a primrose hue; the buttercups were flame-colored. The house was neat and sturdy and, as we dismounted at its stoop, contrived to look hospitable. Melinda marched in first, as we stood looking around and at one another, and threw open windows, talking to herself as she did so. She poked her head out of a second-storey window and said, "Hi! Come in! It's none so bad!" and disappeared again.

She was right. It had been well built, and had survived two years of vacancy with little worse than a few drafts around warped window sills, and a front door that had fallen slightly in its frame and stuck when it was fully closed. The house was a long rectangle, the dividing wall cutting the first floor into two rooms roughly square; the kitchen was at the back and the parlour up front, with a fireplace facing into each room from a central chimney. Upstairs was a hall running half the short length of the house to the chimney, with a bedroom on either side; each had its own tiny fireplace. Up a ladder and through a hole you emerged in a doorway in the peak of the roof, one side of the frame being the chimney again; a wall ran away from you in both directions, cutting the attic in two. The roof sloped sharply on two sides, so the attic rooms were almost triangular; Ger, the tallest of us, could stand up straight only while standing one rung down on the loft ladder.

Everything was beautifully clean; there wasn't a cobweb to be found, and the first two floors were waxed. Melinda grinned at our lavish compliments and said she'd tell them all again to Molly, who had done most of the work, and was young enough still to take pleasure in wild flattery. We laughed and clattered downstairs again, feeling that we had at least one good friend.

Father insisted that we unpack at once, and sleep in our new home. "We thank you, my dear," he said to Melinda, who blushed, "but we have been sleeping on the ground for so long that mattresses on a planed level floor will be a splendid luxury," but we agreed to come to the Griffin for supper.

"You'll save having a lot of people coming here to gawp at you," she said, "when you're trying to get your proper work done." We would also stable our horses there till Father and Ger could repair our own stable. "Your young lady's pony here," Melinda remarked, surveying Greatheart, "needs a barn of his own. The little ones will all love him. He's a giant's horse, just like in the stories us mothers tell them." She petted him, refused to be driven back to town, and set off on foot. "I have to add a little more water to the stew," she said, smiling, "to feed all the extra mouths." Daphne and Rachel were parted reluctantly from the "young lady's pony" and trotted away in their mother's wake.

We were lucky, because everyone in town liked anyone Melinda liked, and everyone was predisposed to like the new blacksmith. Melinda told us that the lack of one had been the chief topic of conversation around the fireplace at the Red Griffin for two years, and if she heard "Ah, what we best need is a proper blacksmith now" once more she would heave a barrel of beer at the speaker.

Ger had the shop going again—bellows mended, the

oven for making charcoal patched air-tight, and tools laid out—within a week of our arrival, while the three of us girls were still airing the bedding, mending socks, and figuring out the whimsical nature of the kitchen ovens. Father spent an afternoon in the stable, measuring and whistling and measuring some more, and in three weeks we had our horses under their own roof; and he was building a pen for them, enlarging the hayloft over them, and thinking about a coop for chickens. Melinda had offered us a few pullets.

We three girls didn't fare quite so well, particularly at the outset; we realized in those first weeks just how spoiled we were, and how unsuited for a life without servants. There's an art to scrubbing a floor; not a very delicate art, but one that must be learned. I, who was a rougher article to begin with, developed calluses almost at once; my sisters' tender skin developed blisters, and the coarse material of our new working clothes chafed them. We didn't talk about our difficulties, beyond the sharing of hints about making things easier that we discovered the hard way; and slowly, as the weeks passed, our darns got less lumpy and our puddings less leaden. We went to bed every night numb with exhaustion, in the beginning, but we grew stronger, and with strength and increasing skillfulness came cheerfulness. Melinda, who almost never stopped talking, had a sharp eye for all of that, and in among her inconsequential chatter she let fall, as if by accident or as among knowing friends, any number of helpful suggestions that we silently though no less appreciatively put to use.

Our first winter was an easy one, the natives told us, and we were as grateful as we could be, although it seemed like a very harsh winter to us. We had never seen more than a few inches of snow on the ground at one time, nor for longer than a few weeks. Greatheart grew a winter coat as thick as a Persian rug, and the long white feathers that grew below his knees entirely covered his huge feet; his short sharp ears were lost in his grey forelock. He was alone in his stable, except for the chickens, since Tom had come through in the autumn, as promised, and collected the two hired horses and the wagon—and complimented us on our progress.

By the time Tom had come and gone I had trained poor Greatheart to go in harness; I was much more conscious of the loss of his dignity than he was, for he had the sweetest of tempers. There wasn't, as it turned out, very much training to it; Ger traded a mended plough for some secondhand harness that could be patched and enlarged to fit our huge horse; and I put it on him and told him to go forwards and he went. He understood almost by instinct the difference in strength and balance of pulling a weight instead of carrying it. Father built a small wagon for him, and Ger strengthened it with iron fastenings and added some ropes and chains for grappling big logs. The horse developed the white marks that come from wearing a collar in the dark dappled grey hair of his shoulders; but perhaps Tom Black had been right, because he did not seem to miss carrying the King.

Even the canary came through the winter in good health and spirits. He was a very useful bird, because he gave Grace and Hope and me something weaker than ourselves to worry over; and he sang as though he appreciated it.

We had had no time to think of a name for him before we left the city, and it was some weeks even after we'd moved into our new home that Hope, putting water in his dish one morning, looked up suddenly and said, "He still doesn't have a name!" Grace and I stared back at her, and then at each other, in dismay. We were silent several minutes, Hope's hand still poised over the water dish; and then the canary, as if impatient, burst into song. We looked at him then, and Grace said, "Of course. Why haven't we thought of it long since? Orpheus." I made an incredulous noise and she smiled and said, "A little sister like you, dear, will upset the best-regulated mind"; and Hope laughed and said, "Orpheus! It's perfect." And Orpheus he became, except that it degenerated over the months to Phooey. I still called him Orpheus, however, and he still sang.

The following summer, a little over a year after we arrived, Gervain and Hope were married. By that time, another room had been added to the house, opening off the parlour, for the newlyweds' bedroom; and the local mason built a chimney for it. Father made them a big bed with a tall scallop-edge headboard for a wedding present. Ger and I had had the two attic rooms, and Grace and Hope had shared one of the bedrooms, while Father had the other. Grace invited me downstairs, but I was fond of my attic, and knew besides that she would like having a room of her own again. There had been a small storm about my being shut off in the attic when we first moved in, but I had insisted. Sharing the little room with my sisters, I said, we'd be as crowded as potatoes in a good chowder; someone had to move upstairs, I was the youngest, and besides I liked the attic.

Father had cut a window for me in the vertical wall,

which overlooked the now re-established garden and beyond that the great forest. When I was not too tired, which happened more often as I grew accustomed to the work, I would stay up an extra hour and read by the light of one precious candle. But candles were too dear to waste often on so profitless a pursuit as reading, even if my eyes didn't soon become too heavy to prop open. I'd been able to keep half a dozen of my oldest, most battered, and most written in books from the auction. In our new life it was the reading I missed the most. The daylight hours were spent working, and much of the evening also, mending clothes and tools and bits of this and that by firelight. "This and that" for most of the spring had consisted of my taking over most of the necessary sewing to free Grace, who was the finer seamstress, to work secretly on an embroidered counterpane for the wedding.

The work had broken down into a routine for each of us. Ger worked in the smithy; his ability was such that before the first winter was past there were people traveling thirty miles to come to him. Father's old skill with wood had gradually returned to his fingers and brain. The tiny lean-to that was built against the blacksmith's shop was enlarged, and Father built carts and cabinets there, and patched roofs and walls in town. His hair had turned snow white, and he moved more slowly than he once had; but he carried himself tall and straight, and he could talk and laugh again. And I suspected Melinda of falling in love with him. He was gentle and courtly to her, as he was to all women, including his daughters; but I thought he displayed a special grace for Melinda. And she, who was simple and kind and forthright, blushed often when he spoke to her, and twisted her hands in her apron like a girl.

Grace and Hope divided the house-work between them, and I did what was left over, the odds and ends that were neither house work nor shop work; and often thought that it would have been much more convenient if I had been a boy—not least because I already looked like one. Ger and I and Greatheart pulled fallen trees out of the eaves of the forest, and Ger taught me to split wood, chop it, and stack it. This was the greatest portion of my work, for there were several fire-places in the house and two more in the sheds to provide fuel for, plus charcoal to cook; and the forge fire, and the kitchen fire, had to burn whatever the weather.

My big horse's strength grew famous, and several times that first year we dragged some undraggable object from where it was stuck fast: an old stump clinging balefully to the soil, a wagon sunk axle deep in spring mud. We also hauled wood for some of the people who lived in town; and in exchange we were sent home with beer and blankets—we were southerners, and correctly presumed tender—and mincemeat pies at the holidays. I never really had time to think about the suitability of my new role, or of how it had come about. I was becoming more boy than girl, it seemed; and perhaps since I was short and plain and had no figure to speak of the townsfolk found my ambiguous position easy enough to accept. The men took their caps off to my sisters, curbed their ribald tongues, and some of them even made rough bows; I was hailed with a wave and a grin, and familiarly called "Beauty." The name had been adopted without the flicker of an eye, so far as I could see: like that of the fierce yellow mastiff who looked after the Red Griffin, who answered, if she was called reverently enough and was in the mood, to the name of "Honey." When Greatheart had hauled yet another malignant old stump out of the ground, and the two of us, plus the owner of the land and all his neighbors, were covered with dirt and splinters, I was clapped on the back and given mugs of small beer.

When spring came I dug up the garden and planted it, and weeded it, and prayed over it, and fidgeted; and almost three years of lying fallow had agreed with it, because it produced radishes the size of onions, potatoes the size of melons, and melons the size of small sheep. The herb border ran wild, and the air smelled wonderful; the breezes often stirred the piney, mossy smell of the forest with the sharp smell of herbs, mixed in the warm smell of fresh bread from the kitchen, and then flung the result over the meadow like a handful of new gold coins. I pruned the apple trees—there were also the remains of an old orchard, and a few of the trees were still productive—and had high hopes of the next winter full of apple jelly.

3

Ger had made us all promise—although I was the only one who had any inclination that needed to be curtailed—never to walk in the woods behind our house without either him or Father for company; the latter reference was courtesy only, because Father was no woodsman. I assumed that Ger meant deep forest, and one afternoon wandered into the first fringe of the big trees with horse and cart, picking up deadwood to be cut up for the house fires; the light scrub that had grown up around the meadow the house sat in had been cut down and burned during our first few weeks here. But Ger saw me from the shop window and came after me, angry; I was surprised to see him angry and explained that I did not mean to disobey orders, and that I was well in sight of the house—indeed, as he had seen me. He relented, but said that he did not want me walking even this near the tall forest trees. This conversation took place during our first autumn, and the leaves were red and gold; it was cold enough already for our breath to hang visible in the air.

He looked up at the tree we were standing under, and sighed. "I'm probably being over-cautious, but I'd rather it were that than fool-hardy." He paused, and rubbed a hand over his chin, considering me. "Have you ever wondered why ours is the only house out this end of town—a full quarter mile from the next house in? And why we take all our drinking water from the well on the hill, when a good stream runs right by the house?"

I stared at him, not expecting mysteries. The stories of the north I had heard in the city had swiftly faded once we had become country dwellers ourselves, and we had been troubled by no goblins. "Not really," I said. "I suppose I thought that the town grew up where it did, and the first smith liked his privacy; and perhaps the stream water isn't good, though good enough to pour over hot iron."

"It's not quite so simple," said Ger, and looked a little

embarrassed. "The story is the wood's haunted. No, not haunted: enchanted. The stream flows out of the forest, as you see, so likely it's enchanted too, if anything is. The first smith—well, tales vary. Perhaps he was a wizard. He was a good smith, but he disappeared one day. He's the one built the house—said he liked the forest, and a forge needs a stream close by, and most of the town gets its water by well. The next smith—the one that left two years ago—dug the well we've got now, to prevent the water's enchanting him; but he didn't like the noises the forest made after dark. Well, forests do make odd noises after dark. Anyway, he left. And they've had some trouble finding someone else. That's how we got this place so cheaply: It's very good for what we had to spend."

"I've never heard anything about all this," I said. "Are you sure you're not making it all up to scare me into obedience? It won't work, you know; it'll only make me mad."

He grinned. "Oh, I'm aware of your temper, Beauty, you needn't fear. And I am telling you the truth—you have the sort of mind that prefers to know things." He said this somewhat wryly; I often pestered him to explain what he was doing and why, when he was using me in the shop; he yielded to my persistence eventually, and

I learned to make charcoal, and could shoe a horse, if the horse co-operated. "I'm also going to ask you not to mention this to your family; your father already knows a bit, but your sisters don't. It'll come up eventually, I suppose, but I'd rather we lived here a little longer and were comfortable here first. It's a good thing for us, we're doing well; it would be a pity to let silly tales scare us." There was a touch of pleading in his voice that surprised me. "I'm just taking a little—precaution."

"Silly tales," I said. "I haven't heard anything about any of this except what you're saying."

"Of course not. Think about it. Blue Hill has wanted a smith; now they've got one, I'll even say a good one, and they don't want to scare him off. After all, if this wood is enchanted, it hasn't done anything in over a hundred years—maybe it's not really enchanted, or maybe it used to be, or maybe it still is, but if we don't disturb it, it won't harm us. And the townsfolk aren't really hiding anything from us; I'm from around here, you know, and Melinda reminded me of this place's history when she wrote me about it." He paused.

"What was it that happened over a hundred years ago?" I asked.

The light was failing fast, and the rays from the

setting sun lit the autumn-colored woods to royal hues, and warmed the dun-colored house to copper. Through the kitchen window I could see a figure in a skirt standing before the fire. Ger took Greatheart's bridle and led him a little way along, following the edge of the forest but moving away from the house.

"Well now," he said at last, and when he glanced at me again his smile was sheepish. "You'll laugh, and I won't blame you. I grew up near here, and the tales you hear in your cradle stay with you whether you will or nay.

"It's said there's a castle in a wild garden at the center of these woods; and if you ever walk into the trees till you are out of sight of the edge of the forest and you can see nothing but big dark trees all around you, you will be drawn to that castle; and in the castle there lives a monster. He was a man once, some tales say, and was turned into a terrible monster as a punishment for his evil deeds; some say he was born that way, as a punishment to his parents, who were king and queen of a good land but cared only for their own pleasure."

"Like the Minotaur," I murmured.

"The which?"

"Minotaur. It's an old Greek legend. What does the monster look like?"

"No two tales agree on that. My mother made me mind her with stories of a bear with foot-long claws; my best friend's mother made him mind because a great boar would come and carry him away on its long tusks if he didn't. And the first owner of the public house here thought it was a griffin. Whatever it is, it must have a mighty appetite. The tale also goes that no hunter ever finds game in there; and you know our garden is curiously free of rabbits and woodchucks—and that in itself is uncanny. And never a deer do you see, and no man has taken one from this forest in the memory of the oldest grandfather's memories of his childhood's tales. There aren't even any squirrels here, and squirrels will live anywhere."

The sun was almost gone now; firelight sent a warm glow through the windows, and left golden footprints in the garden. Father went whistling into the parlour with an arm-load of my afternoon's exertions over the woodpile. He paused at the door and called across to us: "You going back to the shop, Ger? I've not closed up." "Aye," Ger called back. Father went on inside.

"Now, I want your solemn promise," said Ger. "First, that you'll not go scaring your sisters with these stories I've—foolishly, I suppose—told you. And second, that you will stay out of this forest."

I scowled at the ground. I disliked promises on principle because my conscience made me keep them. "I'll say nothing to my sisters," I said, and paused. "If the magic is dangerous to anyone, it's dangerous to you too; I'll stay out if you will."

Ger didn't like that; then he grinned suddenly. "You're half witch yourself, I sometimes think; the forest would probably leave you alone. Okay, I promise. And you?"

"Yes," I said, and went to unload the cart, and put Greatheart away in his stable. Ger was still in the shop when I was finished. He looked up when I entered. "Eh?" he said. "I'll be along in a minute."

"Ger—why did you tell me the story about the forest?"

Ger raised the hammer he was using and studied the signs of wear on its head. "Well now," he said thoughtfully. "I have a very high opinion of your obstinacy; and I knew I'd never get a promise of obedience from you without telling you the truth of it. I'm not a very good liar—and that old forest makes me nervous." He grinned a small boy's grin suddenly and added: "I think it'll be a relief to me to be on my oath to stay out of it; I won't have to think up my own good reasons anymore. Tell your sisters I'll be in in a minute."

• • •

I was awake and sneaking downstairs barefoot before dawn the next morning. I had done a favor for a man who mended harness, and he had said he could fix a soft padded leather collar to go under Greatheart's harness to protect his shoulders; there were two little bald patches beginning that worried me. Bucky had said that it would be ready for me this morning, and it was a longish ride to his farm, and I'd have a lot to do later. And I liked to watch the sun rise.

I saddled Greatheart and led him out, his big feet leaving not-quite-regular saucer marks in the frosty grass. I hesitated as we came to the stream; we usually went around the shop near the stream, then up the little hill towards the town, and I'd haul us water from the well when we rode by it. Today I led the horse to the stream, and waited, watching him: He lowered his head, wrinkled his black nose at the running water, and blew; then he lowered his muzzle and drank. He didn't turn into a frog, nor into a griffin and fly away. He raised his head, slobbering over his last mouthful, and pricked his ears at me without any awareness of having done something out of the ordinary. I walked a pace or two upstream and knelt to scoop up some water with my hands, looping the reins over my wrist. The water was so cold it made my teeth ache with the shock; but it was sweet and very good, better than the dull water from the respectable well. I didn't turn into a frog either, and when I stood up the landscape looked just as it always had. I mounted and we jogged slowly off.

Poverty seemed to agree with me. Grace and I were bridesmaids at Hope's wedding, and while Grace looked fragile and ethereal and Hope was flushed and warm with love, I did contrive to look presentable. After a year of sun and wind and hard work my skin had cleared up, and since I refused to be bothered with a hat, I was brown from working so much outside, which suited me better than my usual sallow pallor. I also stood up straighter since I had had to stop crouching over books; and I was also very strong, although this is not considered an important virtue in a woman. Grace and Hope were exceptional anywhere, but here in the country at least ordinarily pretty girls were outnumbered by plain ones, and I fitted into the background more appropriately than I had in the bright society of the city. I still hadn't grown, though. When I was twelve, my sisters said kindly that the size of my hands and feet indicated that I would grow later; but by this time I was sixteen, and resigned to the fact that that growing streak just wasn't going to arrive. But now that I no longer had to put them in dainty white gloves, I found that my big hands had their uses; and overall I was on pretty good terms with myself. It helped that the only looking-glass in the house was in my sisters' room.

We had worried about Grace the first winter; she seemed never to get over the shock of Robbie's loss, and grew so thin and pale I used to think I could see the firelight shining through her. But with spring she began to recover, and while she was quieter than she once had been, she put on weight, and got some color back in her cheeks. She did most of the work and all of the organizing for the wedding day, and for the feast afterwards; and if she was thinking of Robbie, you would never have known it, seeing her laugh and dance and sing, and watch the level in the punch bowls. She even condescended to flirt a little, very delicately, with the young minister who performed the ceremony; and the poor man went home walking like one drunk, although he had tasted nothing stronger than tea the whole day.

It was the day of the wedding also that Ferdy kissed me, which was how I discovered that looking presentable had its drawbacks. Ferdy was a lad a few years older than myself who helped Ger in the shop when he was needed; Ger said often that the boy had promise as a smith, and he wished he could hire him on a regular schedule. Ferdy was very tall and thin, with bony hands and a big nose and a wild thatch of red hair. We had become friends over the last few months—he'd started working for Ger in early June—and he taught me to fish, and to snare rabbits, and to kill and clean them when they were snared. I liked him, but I didn't like him kissing me.

The wedding day was blue and clear and warm—hot, after the second cup of punch. The ceremony was performed in our tiny parlour, with only the family, and Melinda and a few more special friends; but afterwards the whole town came to the banquet. We had brought the big trestle tables from the Griffin in Greatheart's cart, and set them up in the meadow, and added our own kitchen table; and spread on them were bread and sweet butter, and pies and fruits and jellies, and roast meats, plus the punch, and tea and milk for those who wanted it; and some fiddlers had upon request brought their fiddles, and so there was dancing; and while Ger and Hope laughed at their friends' jokes, and danced with everyone, and thanked them for their good wishes, they never really took their eyes off one another. The day had begun very early, on the understanding that it would end at sundown; tomorrow would be a working day as usual, and it was near harvest, with no time to waste, even on weddings. Grace and Molly and Melinda and I cleaned up afterwards in the young twilight. We agreed with each other that we were exhausted, but none of us could stop smiling.

Ferdy came by the next day especially to see me, though I didn't want to see him, and especially not when he'd made his visit only for that purpose. He apologized to me for the day before, stammering and shaking and turning a bright scarlet, which looked very odd with his orange hair, and he begged that I forgive him. I forgave him to make him stop apologizing; but I also began to avoid him, and when I did come to the shop when he was there, or when he ate the noon meal with us, he followed me with his eyes as if I wore a black hood and carried an axe, and he was next in line.

Ger, who as a new bridegroom shouldn't have been noticing anything but the charms of his new bride, noticed the tension between his assistant and his younger sister-in-law. One day when we were out together hauling wood, and there was the pause between throwing the tools in on the last pile of wood and telling Greatheart to get along there, Ger rubbed his face with a dirty hand and said, "About Ferdy." I stiffened. There was a pause that snickered in my ears, and then Ger said gently, "Don't worry about it. It's different with different people."

I picked up a twig from the forest floor and threw it absently into the wagon. I didn't know what he meant by "it" and I would have died rather than ask him. "Okay," I said. And then as I took hold of Greatheart's bridle I added, "Thanks," over my shoulder, since I knew he was trying to be helpful.

Hope gave birth to twins ten months after the wedding, in May. The girl was born first; Hope named her Mercy, after our sister who had died, although I privately thought that our family already had more than enough virtues personified. The little boy was named Richard, for Ger's father. Mercy was a healthy, happy baby from the beginning, and she was born with golden curls and blue eyes that would look straight at a face bending over her. Richard was puny, bald, and shriveled-looking, didn't eat well, and cried steadily for the first six months; then perhaps he began to feel ashamed of himself, for he cried only at intervals, grew plump and rosy, and produced some reddish-brown hair.

It was in late September that a pedlar from the south came into town and asked at the Griffin if they knew of a man named Woodhouse, or of another, older man named Huston, who used to live in the city. Melinda, after looking him over and asking his business, brought him along to us; and he gave Father a letter with a wax seal.

The letter was from a man named Frewen, whom Father had known and trusted. He was another merchantman who owned several ships, and lived in the city near our old house. He was writing now to say that one of Father's missing ships was returning to port after all: It had been sighted and spoken by one of Frewen's own captains, whose veracity his master would vouch for. Frewen could not say exactly when the ship might reach home; but he hoped to be able to do his old friend Huston the service of holding it for him until he could send word or come himself to dispose of it. He was welcome to stay at Frewen's house while he transacted his business.

Father read the letter aloud to us sitting around the parlour fire after dinner, and a grim silence fell after he was finished. Grace sat as if frozen; if it hadn't been for the firelight she would have been white as milk, her hands clenched into fists in her lap, twisting her apron. Even the babies were quiet; I held Mercy, who looked up at me with big eyes.

"I'll have to go," said Father. Robbie Tucker was an almost tangible presence in the room. "Tom Bradley should be stopping by here any day now; I can go south with them."

And so it was. Tom arrived a week later, and declared himself delighted to have Father's company all the way south to the city again. The letter had cast a pall over all of us that the fine clear autumn weather and the babies' high spirits did nothing to dispel; and it closed down as tightly as a shroud when Father had gone. The worst of it was watching Grace turn cold and white and anxious again, seeing in her a helpless, despairing sort of excitement that she could not quite suppress.

Father told us not to look for him before the spring, when traveling would be easier. But it was a cold night in late March, with the snow nearly a foot thick on the ground after a sudden blizzard, when the front door was thrown open and Father stood on the threshold. Ger strode forwards and caught him in his arms as he staggered, and then half carried him to a seat near the fire. As he sank down with a sigh we all noticed that in his hand he held a rose: a great scarlet rose, bigger than any we had seen before, in full and perfect bloom. "Here, Beauty," he said to me, and held it out. I took it, my hand trembling a little, and stood gazing at it. I had never seen such a lovely thing.

When Father had set out last autumn he had asked us girls if there was anything he could bring us from the city. No, we said: Our only wish is that you should come home to us soon and safely.

"Oh, come now, children," he said. "Pretty girls want pretty things: What little trinkets do you secretly think about?" We looked at one another, not sure what we should say; and then Hope laughed a little and kissed him and said, "Oh, bring us ropes of pearls and rubies and emeralds, because we haven't a thing to wear the next time we visit the King and Queen." We all laughed then, Father too, but I thought his eyes looked hurt; so a little later I said to him, "Father, there is something you can bring me—I'd love to plant some roses here, around the house. If you could buy some seeds that are not too dear, in a few years we'll have a garden that will be the envy of all Blue Hill." He smiled and promised that he would try.

I remembered this now, five months later, the snowcold stem against my fingers. We stood like a Christmas tableau, focused on the huge nodding rose in my hand, snow dripping softly off its crimson petals; then a blast from the still-open door shook us, as it seemed, from sleep. Grace said, "I'll put some water in a cup for it," and went to the kitchen. As I went to close the door, I saw a laden horse standing forlorn in the snow; it raised its head and pricked its ears at me. I hadn't bothered to think that Father must have traveled with some kit besides a scarlet rose. I handed the rose to Grace and said, "I'll see to the horse." Ger followed me, and it happened that I needed his assistance, because the saddle-bags were full and very heavy.

When we returned, Father was sipping some hastily warmed cider, and the silence still lay as thick as the snow outside. Ger and I dumped the leather satchels into a corner near the door, and all but forgot them. As we took our places again by the fire, Hope knelt down in front of Father and put her hands in his lap; and when he looked at her, she said gently: "What has happened since you left us, Father?"

He shook his head. "There's too much to tell it all now. I am tired, and must sleep," and we noticed how old and frail he looked, and his eyes were heavy and sunken. He looked up at Grace: "I am sorry, child, but it was not the *Raven.*" Grace bowed her head. "It was the *Merlyn;* she hadn't been drowned after all." He fell silent again for several minutes, while the firelight chased shadows across his weary face. "I've brought back a little money, and a few things; not much." Ger and I caught each other giving the full saddle-bags puzzled looks; but we said nothing.

Grace had set the rose, now standing in a tall pottery cup of water, on the mantelpiece above the parlour fire. Father looked up at it, and all our eyes were drawn after his. "Do you like it, Beauty, child?" he said. "Yes, indeed, Father," I said, wondering; "I have never seen its like."

He said, as if in a trance, staring at the flower: "Little you know what so simple a thing has cost me"; and as he finished speaking, a petal fell from the rose, although it was unharmed and blooming. The petal turned in the air as it fell, as if it were so feather-light that the warm eddies of air from the fire could lift it; and the firelight seemed to gild it. But it struck the floor with an audible clink, like a dropped coin. Ger bent down and picked it up: It was a bright yellow color. He took it between his fingers, and. with a little effort bent it slightly. "It's gold," he said quietly.

Father stood up as if his back hurt him. "Not now," he said in response to our awed faces. "Tomorrow I will tell you all my story. Will you help me upstairs?" he said to Grace; and the rest of us looked after them when they had gone. Hope banked the fire, and we went our ways to bed. The saddle-bags lay untouched where Ger and I had set them; he gave them hardly a glance as he barred the door.

I dreamed that the stream from the enchanted wood turned to liquid gold, and its voice as it ran over the rocks was as soft as silk; and a great red griffin wheeled over our meadow, shadowing the house with its wings.

Part Two

1

Father was still asleep when the rest of us ate a silent breakfast and started the day's work. After I'd finished eating I went into the parlour to look at the rose again: It was still there—I hadn't dreamed that, at least. The golden petal lay on the mantelpiece where Ger had set it the night before; it teetered gently on its curved base when I looked closely at it, but that must have been a draft in the room. The rose had opened no wider; it was as though it had been frozen at the moment of its most perfect beauty. Looking at it—its perfume filled the whole room—I found it easy to believe that this rose would never fade and die. I went out the front door and shut it softly behind me, feeling that I had just emerged from a magician's cave.

Ger had a skittery colt to shoe that day, and I had promised to help him; so I kept watch through the stable window, as I groomed the horses for the arrival of the colt with its owner. I worked hastily, since I had two horses to finish in the time I usually spent on one; but something about the horse Father had ridden gave me pause. On its rump, near the root of the tail, were five small, round white spots, like saddle- or harness-marks, but nowhere that any harness might wear them. Four were arranged in a curved line, and the fifth was a little space away from the other four, and at a lower angle: like the four fingertips and thumb of a hand. It would have had to be a very big hand, because my fingers, when I tried it, did not begin to reach. As I laid my hand flat on the horse's croup, the animal shivered under the touch and threw its head up nervously. I saw the white of its eye flash as it looked back at me; and it seemed to be in such real fear—it had been quiet and well-mannered till then—that I spent several minutes soothing it.

The skittish colt arrived a little before mid-morning, and I spent a couple of hours hanging on to its headstall and humming tunes in its ear, or holding up the foot diagonal to the one Ger was working on so that it would have too much to do maintaining its balance to cause more trouble.

Father emerged from the house a little before noon, and stood on the front step breathing the air and looking around him as if he had been gone a decade instead of a few months, or as if he were treasuring up the scene against future hardship. As I watched him walk towards the shop I thought that he had recovered remarkably well after only one night's rest; and as he came close enough for me to see him clearly the change seemed more than remarkable. I was distracted from the colt, who promptly lunged forwards; Ger yelled, "Here, hold on now!" and dropped the foot he had picked up. When I glanced guiltily back at him I saw him first notice my father, and the bewilderment I had just felt showed clear on his face.

Father had not just recovered from a tiring journey; he seemed to have lost fifteen or twenty years from his age. Deep lines on his face had been smoothed out, and the squint he had developed as his sight began to fail him was gone, and his gaze was sharp and clear. Even his white hair looked thicker, and he walked with the suppleness of a much younger man.

He smiled at us as though he noticed nothing strange

in our staring, and said, "Forgive me for disturbing you. I hope you don't mind if I spend my first day home just wandering around and getting in my family's way; I promise you I will be back to work tomorrow." We of course assured him he was free to do just as he liked, and he walked out again. There was a pause, while the colt flicked his ears back and forth and suspected us of inventing new atrocities to wreak upon him. "He looks very well, doesn't he?" I said at last, timidly. Ger nodded, picked up a now-cold horse-shoe in the tongs, and put it back in the fire. As we watched the iron turn rosy, he said, "I wonder what's in those saddle-bags?" The mystery was not alluded to again. We finished the colt, and I took him, stepping high in his new shoes and flinging the fast-melting snow around him so that he could shy and dance at the shadows, to the stable and tied him up to await his master's return.

It was after supper that Father finally told his story. We were all sitting around the fire in the front room, trying a little too hard to look peaceful and busy, when Father looked up from his study of the flames: He was the only unoccupied one among us, and the only one who seemed to feel no tension. He smiled around at us, and said: "You have been very patient, and I thank you. I will try to tell you my story now, though the end of it will seem very strange to you." His smile faded. "It seems very strange to me, now, too, as I sit warm and safe among my family." He paused a long time, and the sorrow we had seen in him the night before closed around him again. The rich smell of the rose was almost visible; I fancied it lent a rosy edge to the shadows cast by the firelight. Then Father began the story.

There was pitifully little to tell about his business in the city, he said. The trip south was easy, lasting about seven weeks. He had gone straight to his friend's house upon arrival in town. Frewen had been pleased to see him, and had treated him very well; but despite the man's and his family's kindness, he felt, and he knew he looked, out of place. He had forgotten how to live in the city. The ship had arrived about a week before he had, and its cargo was being held in one of Frewen's warehouses. It would have seemed a very small cargo to him in the days of his prosperity; but with Frewen's help he sold it for a good profit and was able to pay the captain and crew what was owed them, and have a bit left over. The captain, a man named Brothers, was shocked at the change in his master's estate, and was eager to set sail again—the *Merlyn* needed no more than the usual repairs any ten-year-old wooden ship would need after five years at sea—and try and begin to recoup their losses; but Father had demurred. He told Brothers that it was too tall a hill for him to begin to climb again at his age, and while his new life was not so grand as the old had been, still it was a good life, and his family was together.

"It's a curious thing," he said to us musingly; "after the first wrench of having to walk through the town that I had been used to driving in behind a coachman and four, I found I little minded the change. I seem to have developed a taste for country living. I hope I have not been unfair to you, children."

I saw Hope, who was not in Father's line of vision, look down at her slim hands, which were red and rough with work; but she smiled, if a little wryly, and said nothing.

The *Merlyn* was still a sound ship, if not so large and splendid as the ones they were building now, and he set out looking for a buyer for her. He was lucky, and found a purchaser almost immediately, a young captain who sailed for Frewen, who was ready to invest in a small ship of his own. Father had been in town for about a month at that point, and began to think of returning home. He could find out nothing of the *White Raven,* nor of the other ships whose whereabouts had been uncertain and "presumed lost" when we left the city over two years ago. He did hear that ten of the crewmen from the *Stalwart* and the *Windfleet* had arrived home, only about six months ago; and one of the survivors was the third mate who had brought us the story of the little fleet's disaster.

The money he had from the sale of the *Merlyn* made him think of buying a horse and risking the trip north. It had been an easy winter so far, and he was more and more restless, lingering without purpose in the city, eating at Frewen's table and trespassing on his hospitality, when he knew he did not belong. At last he went to Tom Black's stable; and Tom welcomed him and sold him a plain-looking, dependable horse that would be good for the trip, and also be able to earn its keep in Blue Hill. Tom asked after Greatheart, and was very interested, and not at all offended, to hear about the horse's fame as a puller. "I told her he'd do what she told him," he said in a satisfied tone. "Say hello to your family for me, especially the two new little ones."

Father set out only a few days later. He made good time; in less than five weeks he saw smudges of smoke from the chimneys in Goose Landing above familiar hills.

That night stormclouds rolled up, and in the morning it began to snow. He had stayed the night at the Dancing Cat in the Landing, and set off across country soon after dawn. He was sure he couldn't go wrong between there and Blue Hill. He was anxious to get home, and the road would take him some miles out of his way.

The blizzard blew up around him without warning. One minute snow was falling gently over a familiar horizon; the next he was wrapped so closely around in windborne white that he could make out the shape of his horse's ears only with difficulty. They went on now because they could not stop, but they were lost at once.

His horse began to stumble over the ground, as if the footing had suddenly become much rougher. The snow covered everything. He let his mount pick its way as best it could, trying to shield his own face from the sharpslivered wind. He did not know how long he had been traveling when he felt the wind lessen; he dropped his arm and looked around him. The snow was falling only softly now, almost caressingly, clinging to twig-tips, sliding on heaped branches. He was lost in a forest; all he could see in any direction was tall dark trees; overhead he saw nothing but their entangling branches.

In a little while they came to a track. It wasn't much of

a track, being narrow and now deep with snow, presenting itself only as a smooth ribbon of white, a slightly sunken ribbon running curiously straight between holes and hummocks and black tree trunks, straight as if it had been planned and built. A trail of any recognizable sort is a welcome thing to a man lost in a forest. He guided his tired horse to it, and it seemed to take heart, raising its head and picking its feet up a little higher as it waded through the snow.

The track widened and became what might have been a carriage-road, if there had been any reason to drive a carriage through the lonesome forests around Blue Hill. It ended, at last, before a hedge, a great, spiky, hollygrown hedge, twice as tall as a man on horseback, extending away on both sides till it was lost in the darkness beneath the trees. In the hedge, at the end of the road, was a gate, of a dull silver color. He dismounted and knocked, and hallooed, but without much hope; the heavy silence told him there was no one near. In despair, he put his hand to the latch, which fell away from his touch, and the gates swung silently open. He was uneasy, but he was also tired; and the horse was exhausted and could not go much farther. He remounted and went in.

Before him was a vast expanse of silent, unmarked

snow. It was late afternoon, and the sun would soon be gone; just as he was thinking this a ray of sunlight lit up the towers standing above the trees of an orchard that stood at the center of the vast bare field he stood in. The towers were stone, and belonged to a great grey castle, but in the light of the dying sun, they were the color of blood, and the castle looked like a crouching animal. He rubbed his face with his hand and the fancy disappeared as quickly as the red light. A tiny breeze searched his face as if discovering who and what he was; it was gone again in a moment. Once again he took heart; he must be approaching human habitation.

The brief winter twilight escorted him as far as the orchard, and as he emerged from it on the far side, near the castle, his horse started and snorted. An ornamental garden was laid out before him, with rocks, and hedges, and grass, and white marble benches, and flowers blooming everywhere: For here no snow had fallen. He was so weary he almost laughed, thinking this was some trick of fatigue, a waking dream. But the air that touched his face was warm; he threw his hood back and loosened his cloak; he breathed deeply, and found the smell of the flowers heavy and delightful. There was no sound but of the tiny brooks running through the gardens. There were lanterns everywhere, standing on black or silver carved posts, or hanging from the limbs of the small shaped trees; they cast a warm golden light of few shadows. His horse walked forwards as he stared around him, bewildered; and when they stopped again he saw they had come to one corner of a wing of the castle. There was an open door before them, and more lanterns lit the inside of what was obviously a stable.

He hesitated a moment, then called aloud, but got no answer; by now he was expecting none. He dismounted slowly and stared around a minute longer; then he straightened his shoulders and led his horse inside, as if empty enchanted castles were a commonplace. When the first stall he came to slid its doors open at his approach, he only swallowed hard once or twice, and took the horse in. Inside there was fresh litter, and hay in a hanging net; and water that ran into a marble basin from a marble trough, and ran sweetly out through a marble drain; a steaming mash was in the manger. He said "Thank you" to the air in general, and felt suddenly that the silence was a listening one. He pulled the saddle and bridle off the horse, and outside the stall found racks to hang the harness on, which he was sure had not been there when they entered. Except for himself and his horse, the long stable was empty, although there was room enough for hundreds of horses.

The sweet smell of the hot mash reminded him suddenly how hungry he was. He left the stable and shut the door behind him. He looked around, and across the courtyard formed by two wings of the castle, one of which was the stable he had just left, another door opened as if it had been waiting only to catch his eye. He went towards it, giving a look as he passed it to what he supposed was the main entrance: double arched doors twenty feet high and another twenty broad, bound with iron and decorated with gold. Around the rim of the doors was another arch, six feet wide, of the same dull silver metal that the front gates were made of, here worked into marvelous relief shapes that seemed to tell a story; but he did not pause to look more closely. The door that beckoned to him was of a more reasonable size. He went in with scarcely a hesitation. A large room lay before him, lit by dozens of candles in candelabra, and hundreds more candles were set in a great chandelier suspended from the ceiling. On one wall was a fire-place big enough to roast a bear; there was a fire burning in it. He warmed himself at it gratefully, for in spite of the flower garden the enchanted castle was cool, and he was chilled and wet after his long ride.

There was a table set for one, drawn snugly near the fire. As he turned to look at it, the chair, padded with red velvet, moved away from the table a few inches, swinging towards him; and the covers slid off the dishes, and hot water descended from nowhere into a china teapot. He hesitated. He had seen no sign of his host—nor, indeed of any living thing that goes on legs, or wings: There weren't even any birds in the garden—and surely hidden somewhere in this vast pile was the someone who was waited on so efficiently. And one never knew about enchantments; perhaps he, whoever he was, lived alone, and these invisible servants were mistaking this stranger for their master, who would be very angry when he discovered what had happened. Or perhaps there was something wrong with the food, and he would turn into a frog, or fall asleep for a hundred years…. The chair jiggled a little, impatiently, and the teapot rose up and poured a stream of the sweetest-smelling tea he had ever known into a cup of translucent china. He was very hungry; he sighed once, then sat down and ate heartily.

When he was done, a couch he hadn't noticed before had been made up into a bed. He undressed and lay down, and fell immediately into a dreamless sleep.

No more than the usual eight hours seemed to have

passed when he awoke. The day was new; the sun had not yet risen above the tops of the tall, white-crowned forest trees, and a grey but gentle light slipped through the tall leaded windows and splashed on the floor. His clothes had been cleaned, and were folded neatly over the back of the red velvet chair; and for his coarse shirt, a fine linen one had been substituted. His boots and breeches looked new, and his cloak was mysteriously healed of its travel tears and stains. There were tea and toast and an elegantly poached egg on the little table, and a rustcolored chrysanthemum floating in a crystal bowl.

There was still no sign of his host, and he grew anxious. He wanted to be on his way, but he did not wish to leave without expressing his gratitude to someone—and furthermore he still had no idea where he was, and would have liked to ask directions. He went outside, and then into the stable, where he found his horse relaxed and comfortable, pulling at wisps of hay. The tack outside the stall had been cleaned and mended, and the bits and buckles were polished till they sparkled. He went outside again, and looked around; went round the corner of the castle and stared across more gardens, and grassy fields beyond. The snow had disappeared entirely, and the green was the green of early summer. Far across the fields he saw the black border of the wood, and as he strained his eyes something shiny winked at him, something that might be another gate. "Very well," he said aloud. "I will go that way."

He went back into the stable, and saddled the horse, who looked at him reproachfully. He took a last look around the courtyard before riding out, and in a moment of whimsey stood up in his stirrups and bowed to the great front doors. "Thank you very much," he said. "After a night's rest here—at least I'm assuming it was only a night—I feel better than I have in years. Thank you." There was no answer.

He jogged slowly through the gardens. The horse was as fresh and frisky as a youngster, and suited his own light-hearted mood. The thought of the forest held no terror for him; he was certain he would easily find a way out of it; and perhaps tonight he would be with his family again. He was distracted from his pleasant musings by a walled garden opening off the path to his right; the wall was waist-high, and covered with the largest and most beautiful climbing roses that he had ever seen. The garden was full of them; inside the rose-covered wall were rows of bushes: white roses, red roses, yellow, pink, flame-color, maroon; and a red so dark it was almost black.

This arbour of roses seemed somehow different from the great gardens that lay all around the castle, but different in some fashion he could not define. The castle and its gardens were everywhere silent and beautifully kept; but there was a self-containment, even almost a self awareness here, that was reflected in the petals of each and every rose, and drew his eyes from the path.

He dismounted, and walked in through a gap in the wall, the reins in his hand; the smell of these flowers was wilder and sweeter than that of poppies. The ground was carpeted with petals, and yet none of the flowers were dead or dying; they ranged from buds to the fullest bloom, but all were fresh and lovely. The petals he and the horse trampled underfoot took no bruise.

"I hadn't managed to get you any rose seeds in the city, Beauty," Father continued. "I bought peonies, marigolds, tulips; but the only roses to be had were cuttings or bushes. I even thought of bringing a bush in a saddlebag, like a kidnapped baby."

"It doesn't matter, Father," I said.

His failure to find rose seeds for his youngest daughter was recalled to his mind as he gazed at the gorgeous riot before him, and he thought: I must be within a day's journey of home. Surely I could pick a bud—just one flower—and if I carried it very carefully, it would survive a few hours' journey. These are so beautiful: They're finer than any we had in our city garden—finer than any I've ever seen. So he stooped and plucked a bud of a rich red hue.

There was a roar like that of a wild animal, for certainly nothing human could make a noise like that; and the horse reared and plunged in panic.

"Who are you, that you steal my roses, that I value above all things? Is it not enough that I have fed and sheltered you, that you reward me with injustice? But your crime shall not go unpunished."

The horse stood still, sweating with fear, and he turned to face the owner of the deep harsh voice: He was confronted by a dreadful Beast who stood beyond the far wall of the rose garden.

Father replied in a shaking voice: "Indeed, sir, I am deeply grateful for your hospitality, and I humbly beg your pardon. Your courtesy has been so great that I never imagined that you would be offended by my taking so small a souvenir as a rose."

"Fine words," roared the Beast, and strode over the wall as if it were not there. He walked like a man, and was dressed like one, which made him the more horrible, as did an articulate voice proceeding from such a countenance. He wore blue velvet, with lace at the wrists and throat; his boots were black. The horse strained at its bridle but did not quite bolt. "But your flattery will not save you from the death you deserve."

"Alas," said Father, and fell to his knees. "Let me beg for mercy; indeed, much misfortune has come to me already."

"Your misfortunes seem to have robbed you of your sense of honour, as you would rob me of my roses," rumbled the Beast, but he seemed disposed to listen; and Father, in his despair, told him of the troubles he had had. He finished: "It seemed such a cruel blow not even to be able to take my daughter Beauty the little packet of rose seeds she had asked for; and when I saw your magnificent garden, I thought that I might at least take her a rose from it. I humbly beg your forgiveness, noble sir, for you must see that I meant no harm."

The Beast thought for a moment and then said: "I will spare your miserable life on one condition: that you will give me one of your daughters."

"Ah!" cried Father. "I cannot do that. You may think me lacking in honour, but I am not such a cruel father that I would buy my own life with the life of one of my daughters."

The Beast chuckled grimly. "Almost I think better of you, merchant. Since you declare yourself so bravely I will tell you this for your comfort: Your daughter would take no harm from me, nor from anything that lives in my lands," and he threw out an arm that swept in all the wide fields and the castle at their center. "But if she comes, she must come here of her own free will, because she loves you enough to want to save your life—and is courageous enough to accept the price of being separated from you, and from everything she knows. On no other condition will I have her."

He paused; there was no sound but the horse's panting breath. Father stared at the Beast, not able to look away; and the Beast turned from his contemplation of the green meadow, and looked back at him. "I give you a month. At the end of that time you must come back here, with or without your daughter. You will find my castle easily: You need only get lost in the woods around it—and it will find you. And do not imagine that you can hide from your doom, for if you do not return in a month, I will come and fetch you!"

Father could think of nothing else to say; he had a month in which to say good-bye to everything that was dear to him. He mounted with difficulty, for with the

Beast standing so near, the horse was nervous and would not stand still.

As he gathered up the reins, the Beast was suddenly beside him. "Take the rose to Beauty, and farewell for a time. Your way lies there," and he pointed towards the winking silver gate. Father had forgotten all about the rose; he took it in his hand, shrinking, from the Beast; and as he took it the Beast said, "Don't forget your promise!" and he slapped Father's mount on the rump. The horse leaped forwards with a scream of terror, and they galloped across the fields as if running for their lives. The gates swung open as they approached, and they plunged through and into the forest, floundering in the snow until he could pull the poor animal back to a more collected pace.

"I don't remember the rest of that journey very well," said Father. "It started to snow again. I held the reins in one hand, and the red rose in the other. I don't remember stopping until the poor horse stumbled out of the edge of the trees and I recognized our house in the clearing."

Father stopped speaking, and as though he could not look at us, returned his gaze to the fire. The shadows from the restless flames twisted around the scarlet rose, and it seemed to nod its heavy head at the truth of Father's tale.

We all sat stunned, not comprehending anything but the fact that disaster had struck us—again; it was like the first shock of business ruin in the city. It had been impossible to imagine just what losing our money, our home, might mean; but it was numbing, dreadful. This was worse, and we had yet only begun to feel it, because it was Father's life.

I have no idea how long the silence lasted. I was staring at the rose, silent and serene on the mantelpiece, and I heard my own voice say, "When the month is up, Father, I will return with you."

"Oh, *no*," from Hope. "No one will go," said Grace. Ger frowned down at his hands. Father remained staring at the fire, and after a tiny pause, he said: "I'm afraid someone must go, Grace. But I am going alone."

"You are not," I said.

"Beauty—" Hope wailed.

"Father," I said, "he won't harm me. He said so."

"We can't spare you, child," said Father.

"Mmph," I said. "We can't spare you."

He lifted his shoulders. "You would soon have to spare me anyway. You are young, child. I thank you for your offer, but I will go alone."

"I am not offering," I said. "I am going."

"Beauty!" Grace said sharply. "Stop it. Father, why must anyone go? He will not truly come to take you away. You are safe here. Surely you are safe once you are away from his gates."

"Yes, of course," said Hope. "Ger, tell them. Perhaps they'll listen to you."

Ger sighed. "I'm sorry, Hope my dearest, but I agree with your father and with Beauty. There is no escaping this doom."

Hope sucked in her breath with a gasp, then broke out crying. She buried her face in Ger's shoulder and he stroked her bright hair with his hand.

"If it weren't for the rose, I might not believe it. . . . I blame myself for this; I should have warned you better," Ger said very low. "There have been stories about the evil in that wood for generations; I should not have ignored them."

"You didn't," I said. "You told us to stay out of it, that it was old and dangerous, and there were—funny stories about it."

"There was nothing you could have done, lad," said Father. "Don't worry yourself about it. It was my own fault for taking a foolish risk in bad weather. My own fault, none other's; and none other shall pay for it."

Grace said: "Funny stories. Hope and I heard stories about a monster who lived in the forest, a creature that lived in the forest and ate everything that walked or flew, which is why there is no game in it. And how it likes to lure travelers to their deaths . . . and it's very, very old, as old as the hills, as old as the trees in its forest. We never mentioned it to the rest of you because we thought you'd laugh; Molly told us about it. To warn us to stay out of the wood." I looked over at Ger. The stories he'd told me two years ago had never been mentioned again.

Hope had stopped crying. "Yes, we thought it was all foolishness; and we needed no urging to stay out of that awful wood," she said. The tears began to run down her cheeks again; but she sat up and leaned against Ger, who put his arm around her. "Oh, Father, surely you can stay here."

Father shook his head; and Ger said abruptly: "What's in your saddle-bags?"

"Nothing very grand. A little money, though; I thought we might buy a cow, instead of having to bring milk from town for the babies, and—well, there's probably not enough."

Ger stood up, still holding Hope's hand, then knelt by the leather bags, still piled in their corner. Grace and

Hope, usually the most conscientious of housekeepers, had for some reason let them lie untouched. "I noticed when Beauty and I brought them in yesterday that they were very heavy."

"They were? They aren't—I mean, they can't be. I didn't have all that much." Father knelt beside Ger and unbuckled the top of one and threw back the flap. Dazed, he lifted out two dozen fine wax candles, a linen tablecloth with a delicate lace edge, several bottles of very old wine and a bottle of even older brandy, and a silver corkscrew with the head of a griffin, with red jewels for eyes that looked very much like rubies; and wrapped in a soft leather pouch was a carving knife with an ivory handle cut in the shape of a leaping deer, with its horns laid along its straining back. At the bottom of the bag, piled wrist deep, were coins: gold, silver, copper, brass. Buried among the coins were three small wooden boxes, and inlaid on each of their polished lids was an initial in mother-of-pearl: G, H, and B. "Grace, Hope, and Beauty," said Father, and handed them to us. In my sisters' boxes were golden necklaces, and ropes of pearls, diamonds, emeralds; topaz and garnet earrings; sapphires in bracelets, opals in rings. They made a shining incongruous pile in laps of homespun.

My box was filled to the brim with little brownish,

greenish, irregularly shaped roundish things. I picked up a handful, and let them run through my fingers, and as they pattered into the box again I laughed suddenly, as I guessed what they must be: "Rose seeds!" I said. "This Beast has a sense of humour, at least. We shall get along quite well together, perhaps."

"Beauty," Father said. "I refuse to let you go."

"What will you do then, tie me up?" I said. "I *will* go, and what's more, if you don't promise right now to take me with you when the time comes, I will run off tonight while you're asleep. I need only get lost in the woods, you said, to find the castle."

"I can't bear this," said Hope. "There must be a way out."

"No; there is no way out," said Father.

"And you agree?" asked Grace. Ger nodded. "Then I must believe it," she said slowly. "And one of us must go. But it need not be you, Beauty; I could go."

"No," I said. "The rose was for me. And I'm the youngest—and the ugliest. The world isn't losing much in me. Besides, Hope couldn't get along without you, nor could the babies, while my best skills are cutting wood and tending the garden. You can get any lad in the village to do that."

Grace looked at me a long minute. "You know I always wear you down in the end," I said.

"I see you are very determined," she said. "I don't understand why."

I shrugged. "Well, I'm turned eighteen. I'm ready for an adventure."

"I can't—" began Father.

"I'd let her have her way, if I were you," said Ger.

"Do you realize what you're saying?" shouted Father, standing up abruptly and spilling the empty leather satchel off his lap. "I have seen this Beast, this monster, this horror, and you have not. And you are willing that I should give him—*it*—my youngest daughter, your sister, to spare my own wretched life!"

"You are the one who does not understand, Papa," I said. "We are not asking that I be killed in your stead, but that I be allowed to save your life. It is an honourable Beast at least; I am not afraid." Father stared at me, as if he saw the Beast reflected in my eyes. I said: "He cannot be so bad if he loves roses so much."

"But he is a Beast," said Father helplessly.

I saw that he was weakening, and wishing only to comfort him I said, "Cannot a Beast be tamed?"

As Grace had a few minutes before, Father stared

down at me as I sat curled up on the floor with the little wooden box in my lap. "I always get my own way in the end, Papa," I said.

"Yes, child, I know; and now I regret it," he said heavily. "You ask the impossible, and yet—this is an impossible thing. Very well. When the month is up, we will go together."

"You won't see your roses bloom," murmured Hope.

"I'll plant them tomorrow. They're enchanted too— if I'm lucky, maybe I will see them," I said.

2

That night I couldn't sleep. Father had gone upstairs immediately after he agreed to let me go to the castle with him in a month's time; he had said no further word, and I followed him up the stairs only a few minutes later, fearing questions, and sensing an ominous quiver in the silence.

I sat on my bed and looked out at the quiet woods, black and silver in snow and moonlight, and serene. There was nothing watchful or brooding about that stillness; whatever secrets were hidden in that forest were so perfectly kept that their existence could not be suspected nor even imagined by any rational faculty.

I had been granted my wish; I would go and claim the Beast's promise to take the daughter in the father's place. Grace's question came back to me, and the beaten look on Father's face: Why was I so determined? "I wish I knew," I said aloud. I believed that my decision was correct, that I and no other should fulfill the obligation; but a sense of responsibility, if that was what it was, did not explain the intensity of my determination.

I had brought the little wooden box with my initial on it upstairs with me. I poured its contents onto my bed; the tiny dark drops gleamed dully in the moonlight as they clattered one over another. The last thing to fall out of the box was bigger, an icy yellow under the pale light, and it bounced and rang as it landed, spraying seeds across the bed. I picked it up. It was a ring, shaped like a griffin, like the silver handle of the corkscrew downstairs. But this griffin was gold, and it had its mouth open, with diamond fangs glittering cold, and its wings spread: The wings were the band that fitted around the finger; they overlapped at the back, next to the palm of the hand. The creature was rearing up, claws stretched out. It looked fine and noble, with its neck arched and its head thrown back, the line of its body making a taut and graceful curve. It did not look evil, nor predatory; it was proud, not vicious. I put it on my finger, which it fitted perfectly, and hastily scooped the seeds back into the brown box. I would have only a few hours of sleep now, and I could ill afford to waste a day by being tired—especially after tonight, I thought, my hand pausing as I closed the lid. Especially during my last four weeks. Three weeks and five days.

I dreamed of the castle that Father had told us about. I seemed to walk quickly down long halls with high ceilings. I was looking for something, anxious that I could not find it. I seemed to know the castle very well; I did not hesitate as I turned corners, went up stairs, down stairs, opened doors; nor did I linger to look at the wonderful rooms, the frescoed ceilings, the paintings on the walls, the carved furniture. My sleeping self was dazzled, bewildered; but the dream self went on, more and more anxious, till I awoke shivering with the first light of dawn fingering my face. I dressed hurriedly, hesitated, looking at my hand, then pulled the ring off and hid it under my pillow; a needless gesture since no one but myself ever entered my little attic room. I finished lacing my boots as I went downstairs—two activities that did not mix well, and I had to do my boots all over again when I sat down at the kitchen table.

The same uneasy silence that had characterized

Father's first day home continued; but with a difference. Yesterday we had feared a doom we did not know; today the doom was known by us all, and feared no less. No one spoke at breakfast except the babies, and I left the table first.

I frowned at the ground outside. Most of the snow from the blizzard Father had been lost in had melted quickly under yesterday's warm sun, and from the warm touch of the morning wind on my cheek I thought that what remained would soon disappear; but the ground was still much too hard to be planting anything. Nor, if I managed to chop a few holes, would the seeds be likely to find the cold earth very hospitable. They're magical, after all, I thought. I'll do what I can.

I borrowed a pick from Ger, and fetched a spade from my gardening tools, and set to work cutting a narrow, shallow trench around the house, close to the outside wall where perhaps the ground was a little warmer than in the meadow or the garden. By lunchtime I was tired and sweating, but I had sprinkled my seeds in the trench and covered them over roughly; and had a few left to bury along one wall of the stable and one wall of the shop. No one said anything to me, although I should have been tending the animals and chopping wood.

At the noon meal Grace said, "I can't just ignore what we decided—or what Beauty decided for us—last night, as we all seem to be trying to do. Beauty, child, I won't try to dissuade you—" She hesitated. "But is there anything we can do?" Anything you'd like, perhaps, to take with you?" The tone of her voice said that she felt she was offering me silk thread to build a bridge across a ravine.

"It will be so lonesome," said Hope, timidly. "Not even any birds in the trees." The canary was singing his early-afternoon-on-the-threshold-of-spring song.

There was a pause while I stared at my soup and thought: There isn't anything I want to take. The clothes I stand up in, and one change—about all I've got anyway. They can keep the dress I wore to Hope's wedding, and cut it up and use it for baby clothes. The skirt I wear to church will fit either of my sisters with just a little alteration. If the Beast wants me to look fine, he'll have to produce his own tailor. I thought of Father's description of velvet and lace; and it occurred to me that in my dream I had been richly dressed in rustling embroidered skirts and soft shoes. I could almost feel those shoes on my feet, instead of my scratched and dirty boots. I was still staring at my soup, but I saw only beans and onions and carrots; I rearranged the pattern with my spoon.

Ger said: "Greatheart will be a little company for her, at least."

I looked up. "I had hoped to ride him there, but I'll send him back with Father. You need him here."

"Nay, girl," said Ger in an inflection not his own, "he'll not eat if you go off and leave him. He goes with you."

I put down my spoon. "Stop it, Ger, don't tease me. I can't take him. You need him here."

"We'll get along without," Ger said in his own voice. "We have an extra horse now, don't forget, and we can buy another if we need it—with the money your father brought back from the city. They won't be Greatheart's equal, but they'll do us."

"But—" I said.

"Oh, do take him," Hope said. "It'll seem like we haven't quite forsaken you, if you have your horse." She stopped abruptly, and fiddled with her napkin.

"He is your horse, you know," said Ger. "For all his sweet ways it's you he watches for, and listens to. I won't say he wouldn't eat, but he'd perform no prodigies for me or any of the rest of us. He'd just be a big strong horse."

"But—" I said again, uncertainly. I could feel my first tears pricking my eyes; I realized that I would feel much less desolate if I could keep Greatheart with me.

"Enough," said Father. "I agree with Hope: Your keeping your horse will comfort *us* at least. If you were a little less stubborn, girl, you'd be comforted too." A little more gently he added: "Child, do you understand?"

I nodded, not trusting myself to speak, and picked up my spoon again. The tension was broken; we were a family again, discussing the weather; and the work to be done in the coming weeks—and the necessary preparations for the youngest daughter's coming journey. We had accepted it and could begin to cope with it.

Those last few weeks passed very quickly. The knowledge that I was leaving changed the tenor of all our lives very little, once we had adjusted to the simple fact of it. The story we devised for the town's benefit was that an old aunt, nearing the end of her life and finding herself without heir, had offered to take one of us in; and it was decided that I would benefit most (and could best be spared from home), because I would be able to take up my studies again. All our friends were sorry to hear I was leaving, but were glad of what they thought would be a "grand chance" for me—even the ones who had scant respect for book learning were polite if not cordial, for my family's sake. Melinda said, "You must come visit us when you're home for a holiday—she'll let you come home for a spell, sometimes, surely?"

"Oh yes—please come see us," put in Molly. "I want to hear all about the city." Melinda sniffed; she didn't approve of cities, nor of wanting to hear about them. She felt that we had survived our lengthy exposure very well, considering, and while she approved of my going because she recognized the claims of things like aunts, it was still an unfortunate risk.

"She's seen the city before," Melinda said drily, and Molly flushed: They'd been careful not to ask us what life in the city was like, since we had left it under such unhappy circumstances. "We wish you well, in all events, Beauty," Melinda continued. "But before we leave, say that you will come say hello to us when you come back to visit your family."

"I will if I can," I said uncomfortably. "Thank you for all your good wishes."

Melinda looked a little surprised at my answer and remarked to no one in particular; "Is this aunt such an ogre then?" and kissed me, and she and Molly left to go home. We were in the kitchen, Father smoking a pipe and looking thoughtful, Grace peeling potatoes, Hope feeding the babies; I was mending the throat latch of Greatheart's bridle. Ger was still in the shop. We had never discussed just how long I would be gone—the Beast's words led one to believe that it would be forever, which didn't bear thinking of, so we didn't think of it.

To break the silence I said, "This ogreish aunt may not be a complete fiction after all. I probably shall be able to get on with my studies: He must have a library in that great castle of his. He must do something with the days besides guard his roses and frighten travelers."

Father shook his head. "You cannot know; he is a Beast."

"A Beast who talks like a man," I said. "Perhaps he reads like a man too."

Grace finished slicing the potatoes and put them in the skillet where onions were frying. I had grown very fond of fried potatoes and onions since we'd left the city, I wondered if I would get any at the castle. I would have refused such a humble dish five years ago, if our cook could ever have thought of offering us such a thing.

"Beauty, you assume that everyone must be like you," said Grace. "There are a lot of us who find reading more a burdensome task than anything else. Never mind Latin and Greek and so forth."

"I could almost feel sorry for this Beast," said Hope

cheerfully, wiping tomato soup from Richard's chin. "I still remember Beauty trying to teach me declensions, which I had no desire to learn." The potatoes were sizzling.

"Stop it," said Father harshly; and Ger came in just then, so no more was said. He handed me a thin piece of leather. "Thought this might help. That strap has about reached the end of its usefulness."

"Thanks," I said.

"Supper," said Grace.

Winter began to slide away from us in good earnest; the blizzard Father had come home in seemed to be the last of the year, and spring arrived to take charge. The brook from the forest tore off the ice that had built up along its banks and hurled it downstream with the strength of the seasonal high water. The track from house to shop to stable turned to mud. Grace swept the kitchen and parlour floor twice a day, and I couldn't keep Greatheart's stockings white, and spent a lot of time sponging the mud off his grey belly and leather harness.

For three weeks there was no sign of my roses; I worried that perhaps the seeds would be washed away in the churned-up mud, because I hadn't been able to bury them very deeply; and told myself often and with increasing sternness as time passed that I had been a complete fool to try to plant them so early. I told myself that they were lost now and would do no one any good, and all was due to my own stupid folly in supposing that even magical seeds could grow at this time of year.

The rose on the mantelpiece stayed as fresh and bright as it had been when Father first handed it to me. It dropped no more petals; it didn't even drink much water. Grace had put it in a tall crystal vase from among the lovely things that had been found so mysteriously in Father's saddle-bags, and taken the pottery cup it had first rested in back to the kitchen.

Then, seven days before we were to ride into the forest, I found three little green shoots along one stable wall. I stared at them, sucking in my breath, and ran back to the house to look for more. I found at least a dozen, in a straight little row under the kitchen window that faced the forest. They weren't weeds, I was sure, although I had wished so hard for some sign of my roses that I could almost believe that I was imagining things. There were a few more along the front of the house, and I found what I thought might be two more of the same thin tender green bits poking their heads tentatively above ground outside the shop. It was morning, and I had been on my way to curry and feed the horses. When I went back to the stable, I saw *five* little green sprouts. I must have over-looked the last two.

Returning to the house for the noon meal, I found a whole regimental line of short green spikes lined up by the wall of the house looking towards the forest; some of them were quite three inches high. "My roses!" I yelled through the kitchen door. "Come see my roses!"

They grew so fast those last few days that I found myself watching them out of the corners of my eyes as if I would catch them at something: hastily unrolling a leaf, threading a new runner up the vines that were joyously climbing the sides of the house, shop, and barn. The seedlings nearest the forest did the best, as if there were some radiated strength emanating from their place of origin. On the fifth day there were tiny buds beginning; on the sixth day the buds swelled till touches of color, red or pink, could be seen at their tips. Father and I would ride away the morning of the next day.

Like the night following the telling of Father's fantastic story, again on my last night at home I found myself unable to sleep. After supper I had gone outside again, oppressed by the unspoken tension indoors, and walked around the meadow. The stream's voice was almost articulate, but I couldn't quite catch the words; and I felt that I was being taunted for my dulness. The pebbles on the banks of the stream watched me knowingly. I went to the stable, although I knew everything was in military order there, the appropriate tack cleaned ruthlessly and laid out for tomorrow's journey. I had groomed Greatheart till he gleamed like polished marble, and combed his long mane and tail over and over again till he must have wondered what was wrong with me. He had been a little uneasy the last few days, as uneasy as a great placid horse can be, sensing some change in the air. At least he knew where I was when I was shining him; he put his head over the door and pointed his ears at me with a little anxious quiver of his nostrils when I blew the lantern out and left him at last. "Don't worry," I said, "you're coming too," and closed the barn door as he watched me. The moon was three-quarters full, and there were just a few little, dancing clouds in the sky. The forest was quiet, except for the sounds that trees make.

I went up to bed immediately, pausing downstairs only long enough to nod to everyone, sitting around the fire in the front room with their hands busy, although it was past the usual hour that we all went to bed, and to hang the lantern on its hook by the door. "You're all ready?" Ger asked quietly. "Yes," I said. "Good night."

I paused on the second floor at the foot of the ladder to my loft. The forest looked different here. I was used to looking at it from my attic, or from ground level. The difference intrigued me, and I leaned out the window, teasing myself that there was an important difference, philosophical or moral, instead of just the fact of a few extra feet up or down, a change of physical perspective. There was a murmur of voices from downstairs. Suddenly I heard clearly, without wanting to.

"Poor Ferdy," said Ger. "I told him he needn't come till afternoon tomorrow." Ger's wish to hire the boy full time, so that he could teach him the smith's trade, was about to be fulfilled: Ferdy would work here daily, dividing his time between the shop and wood-cutting. He'd be invited to live here, once I was gone, probably in Ger's old attic room, since Hope had said loudly, when we had discussed his staying here, "Of course we'll leave Beauty's room alone."

Like the rest of the townspeople, Ferdy had been told three weeks ago that I was leaving. Ger had told him in the shop while I was there too, holding another fractious horse while it was shod. Ferdy had listened in silence, and had remained silent for several minutes after Ger was finished. Then he said: "I wish you good luck, Beauty," and little else, either that day or in the weeks following. He avoided me with much more purpose than I had ever expended in avoiding him, and he no longer ate dinner with us.

"Poor Ferdy," agreed Hope.

The roses had clambered all around the window; there was an especially fat bud resting on the sill, its tip showing maroon. I took my boots off and climbed the ladder silently.

But I couldn't sleep. What little packing I had to do—my books, a few clothes—was done; the saddle-bag sat on the floor waiting to be carried downstairs at first light and tied on Greatheart's back. I wrapped myself in a blanket and curled up at the head of my bed, where I could lean against the wall and stare out the window. I hadn't worn the griffin ring since the first night, but I had begun carrying it in a pocket. I found that I didn't like leaving it in my room, that I kept thinking about it; I was comforted in some obscure fashion when I carried it with me: It was a token of my future; I read it as a good omen. I felt for it now, pulled it out, and put it on.

I must have dozed at last, because I found myself in the castle again, walking through dozens of handsome, magnificently furnished rooms, looking for something.

I had a stronger sense of sorrow and of urgency this time; and also a sense of some other—presence; I could describe it no more clearly. I found myself crying as I walked, flinging doors open and looking inside eagerly, then hurrying on as they were each empty of what I sought. I woke abruptly; the sun was rising. The first thing I saw was three roses, opening in the faint light. Two were the dark red of the rose on the mantelpiece, one was white, delicately veined with peach color. I hadn't realized the vines had reached so high. Two of the roses nodded gently, visible only barely above the window sill, but the third had wound up the side and hung at eye level, as I stood looking out, bowing on its stem as if it were looking in the window at me. I opened the window and leaned out, and to my exquisite delight found that the whole side of the house was covered with roses in full bloom; and I could see bright flowers leaning against the shop and stable walls. "Thank you," I whispered to no one.

I closed the window again and hurried into my clothes; today I left the griffin ring on my finger. The wooden box that had held the rose seeds was packed away in the saddle-bag. I made my bed neatly, or as neatly as I was capable of, smoothing the blankets with greater care than I ever used; and I hesitated, looking around, before I climbed down the ladder for the last time. The old wooden trunk was pushed into one corner; the bed stood along the long wall, under the eaves. My few books were gone from the opposite wall, where they had lain heaped on the floor near the little window. The big red rose was tapping softly against the window with a sound of velvet rubbing against glass. On an impulse I went across and opened the window again, and broke the stem; the rose fell graciously into my hand. I closed the window then and went downstairs without looking back, the saddlebag over my shoulder and the rose held respectfully in one hand.

I met Grace in the garden, returning to the house with her apron full of eggs. She gave me as much of a smile as she could summon, and said, "There's a bit of butter to fry these in." Butter we used only on special occasions.

By the time I had saddled Greatheart and Father's horse the sunlight was winning a way through the light frost on the ground. I tucked the rose I had plucked under the crownpiece on Greatheart's bridle and went in to breakfast. I came in silently through the front door so that I could stand in the parlour alone for a few minutes and look around me. The rose on the mantelpiece was dying at last: The petals were turning brown and many had dropped off; the stem was withered. The one golden petal glinted through the dry brown ashes. I could hear the rest of the family in the kitchen.

Breakfast was a silent meal. As soon as I could I escaped to the stable. I paused with my hand on the kitchen door and said to Grace, "The eggs were delicious." She gave me a stricken look, then said, "Thank you," to the pile of dirty dishes she was holding.

Greatheart was anxious to get to whatever it was that was ruining my peace and therefore his. He came out of his stall with a rush, pulling me with him and nearly wrenching my shoulder out of its socket. He tossed his head, making the rose on his headstall bounce, and pranced a few steps, no mean feat for a horse of his bulk. Odysseus, Father's horse, was tamer. I looped his reins over one arm while I wrestled with Greatheart. The stupid animal actually tried to rear, and lifted me several inches off the ground; he recollected himself before he went too high, and returned to earth, looking sheepish. The rest of the family was collected by the kitchen door. Grace and Hope stood at the threshold, each with a baby in her arms. Father and Ger stood a step lower, on the little patch of bare ground between the door and the gate in the fence around the garden. The roses were a blaze of vivid color, lighting up the dun-colored house, the plain clothes, and the white faces.

Ger came to where we stood and took Greatheart's bridle. The big horse arched his neck and quivered, but he stood still. "I'll hold him for a bit while you—" he said, and stopped. I nodded. Father took Odysseus's reins, and I walked slowly to where my sisters were standing. "Well," I said, and kissed them and the babies in turn. Mercy and Richard didn't know what was going on, but everyone looked solemn and rather terrible, so they looked solemn too. Mercy stuffed most of one fist in her mouth, and Richard was inclined to cry; he was whimpering, and Hope rocked him gently. "Good-bye," I said. My sisters said nothing. I turned and walked back towards the horses; Father was already mounted. Greatheart was watching me, and as I turned towards him gave a great bound forwards, and I saw the blacksmith's muscles on Ger's arms stand out as he tried to hold him. Greatheart subsided, sinking back on his hocks, and chewing on his bits till the white foam splashed to the ground.

"Oh," I said, turning back to my sisters. "All the stuff in Father's saddle-bags: I hope you'll use it. It's not—I mean, I wish you would," I ended lamely. They both nodded. Grace gave me a ghost of a smile; Hope blinked, and a big tear rolled down her cheek and splashed onto Richard's face. He broke into a thin cry. I still hesitated. "Use all that fine silver on my birthday," I said at last, not having thought of what I wished to say, or how to say it; and turned away hastily.

Greatheart was throwing his head up and down, but he was otherwise quiet: Ger embraced me with his free arm and kissed my forehead. "I'll toss you up," he said. The horse stood as still as a stone for this operation, and heaved a great sigh as I settled in the saddle. I reached forwards to fix the rose a little more firmly. "Okay?" I said to my father. He nodded. Ger stepped back.

I turned Greatheart towards the forest edge, and he paced forwards deliberately, quiet now, and Odysseus followed. Just before I reached the trees I turned in the saddle to wave; Ger raised a hand in reply. I nudged the horse into a trot, and we broke into the first line of trees. The last thing I heard as the forest closed around Father and me was Richard's small forlorn wailing. I urged Greatheart into a canter, and the noise of the horses crashing through the underbrush drowned everything else.

When I pulled him up at last the edge of the forest

was no longer visible; I could see nothing but tall trees in every direction. Few of them were small enough for me to have reached all the way around them and touched fingertips to fingertips. The scrub at the beginning of the forest had thinned out; there was moss underfoot now, and I saw a few violets, a few tardy snowdrops, and some tiny yellow flowers I didn't recognize. It was cool here without being cold; sunlight dripped a little way among the leaves, but without warmth. Most of the tree trunks were straight and smooth to a height above our heads, where the broad branches began. I heard water running somewhere; except for that, and the noises of our passage—harness jingling and squeaking and occasional patches of cobweb ice that shattered underfoot—the woods were perfectly still. Father was a little way behind me. I looked up and could see little bits of blue sky, like stars against the variegated green and black and brown. I breathed deeply and for the first time for several days I felt my heart lift out of my boots and take its proper place in my breast. As Father jogged up beside me I said, "This is a good forest." He smiled and said, "You don't lack courage, child."

"No, I mean it," I said.

"Then I'm glad. I find it a bit oppressive, myself,"

he said, looking around him. We went on a few more minutes, and then he said, "Look." I could see something pale among the trees. In another minute I recognized it: It was the road leading to the heart of the forest, and the castle.

Part Three

❧ 1 ❧

I was eager to make as much speed as possible; I knew that Father was on the brink of begging me to turn back and let him go on to the castle alone. I would not leave him, whatever he said now, but I was uncertain just how far beyond this essential determination my thin courage could bear me. I knew I would go on, but I wanted to do it with dignity; if Father said anything it was likely that I would cry, and then the journey would be a great deal more miserable than it was at present, with nothing more dreadful between us than the grim and thoughtful silence that we shared. I kept hearing Richard's tiny crying in my mind, and seeing the gorgeous roses framing Grace and Hope and Ger as they faced the forest. I tried to feel encouraged by my sense that the forest was welcoming, not hostile, but that shallow cheerfulness seemed to ebb away as we walked onto the white road. I prodded Greatheart into a trot, and Father fell a little behind again; for a little while I didn't have to worry about the expression on my face. I could feel that it wasn't one I wanted him to see.

We stopped once to rest the horses; neither of us was hungry, although there was food in our saddle-bags. It was a little after noon when we saw the dense dark hedge and the huge silver gate looming up before us. The gates shimmered like a mirage in sea-fog. Odysseus, who had been well-behaved until now, shivered and shied, and did not want to go near those tall silent gates. At last Father dismounted and led the unhappy horse to the gates, but when he put out his hand to touch them, Odysseus reared and broke away. He stopped again only a few feet from Father's outstretched hand, looking back over his shoulder, ashamed of himself but still afraid. Greatheart stood still and watched.

"Father," I said, as he stroked his horse's nose and tried to calm him, "you needn't come any farther with me. These are the gates to the castle. If you leave at once you will be home by suppertime." My voice cracked only a very little. I was glad I could sit quietly on Greatheart, that I did not have to dismount and make my legs carry me, and that I could hide my shaking hands in the thick white mane that fell over his withers.

"Child—you must go back. I cannot let you do this—I cannot think what made me agree to it in the first place. I must have been mad to think that I could let you go—like this."

"The decision is long past now—you cannot revoke it; and you agreed because you had no choice." I swallowed, although my mouth was dry, and went on before he could interrupt: "The Beast won't harm me. And perhaps, after all, he is only testing our sense of—fair play. Perhaps I won't have to stay long." The words sounded well, but my voice didn't, and neither of us believed what I was saying. I hurried on. "Go. Please. Parting will only be worse later." I thought: I couldn't bear to see this Beast *send* you away. "I'll be all right." I rode towards the gates, but before I had wheeled Greatheart so that I could touch them with my hand, they swung open without a sound, and a trackless field of bright green grass lay before me. "Good-bye, Father," I said, half-turning in my saddle. Father had remounted. Odysseus was standing still, but the stiffness in his neck and ears indicated his tension and fear. One gesture from Father would send him plunging back down the road the way we had come.

"Good-bye, dear Beauty," he said almost inaudibly. My ears rang with my heartbeats. I rode forwards before he could say any more, and the gates of mist closed impassively behind me. I turned and faced forwards before they were quite shut, and did not look back again.

Sunlight and the smell of the sweet grass were better than sleep or food; I felt that I was awakening from a dream left behind in the shadowed eaves of the forest. When we came to the edge of the orchard we found a white pebbled path leading between the trees towards the castle.

I cannot begin to describe the gardens. Every leaf and blade of grass, or pebble in the path, or drop of water or flower petal, was perfect, in plan and in execution: true in color and in shape, unworn, and unharmed as if each had been created only a moment ago, as if each were a gem, and the polish of each facet the life's work of a fairy jeweler. I clung to Greatheart's mane as he went forwards at a gentle walk; the motion of his shoulders and flanks seemed like the heaving of a ship in storm.

The castle rose up before us like sunrise, its towers

and battlements reaching hundreds of feet into the sky. It was of grey stone, huge block set on block; but it caught the sunlight like a dolphin's back at dawn. It was as big as a city, I thought; not one building, but many, tied together by corridors and courtyards; I stared around at what I could see of the wings and walls of it stretching in many directions. I could not begin to imagine the number of rooms it must contain. But it stood silent, the windows dark, apparently deserted. But not quite deserted, I told myself unhappily. Oh dear.

Greatheart came to a halt before the stable, whose door had slid back at our approach. Inside, afternoon sunlight slanted through tall narrow windows with half-moons of stained glass set in their arched tops. The colored glass held pictures of horses, standing, galloping, richly caparisoned or free of harness, with long waving manes and bright dark eyes. The bits of color sprinkled the marble walls of the stalls and the smooth golden sand of the floor. The door to the first stall slid back, just as it had for Father, as we approached, and straw finished scattering itself into the corners as we looked in. Greatheart pricked his ears at self-propelled bedding; but when I pulled his bridle off he quickly transferred his attention to the mixed grain in the manger. He did not eat so well at home.

There was a selection of bone-handled brushes, combs, and soft cloths on a shelf on the stall's outer wall. I groomed the horse carefully, but still I lingered; I did not want to be finished, to leave him in the stable and go by myself into the castle, where the Beast was doubtless waiting for me. The Beast had said that no harm would come to me, but how did I know? I thought of how ready I had been to believe those promises of safety when I had first heard Father's tale, beside our own hearth. He was only a Beast. What could he possibly want with me anyway? I banished that thought as I had many times before in the past month. I recalled unhappily the tales of the insatiable monster that lived in the forest and ate all the game. Perhaps the Beast found young maiden a difficult dish to procure, and had to resort to trickery. I had cut and carried too much wood in the last two and a half years to make a very delicate morsel; but this was no comfort, since it would undoubtedly be discovered too late.

I remembered that Father's tack had been mysteriously cleaned while it hung on a rack overnight. The rack I found, it having conjured itself outside the stall while I was in it. "Won't you let me wash it myself? " I said to the air, looking up as if expecting to see something looking down; I lowered my gaze hastily and was unnerved by the appearance of a bucket of warm water, soap, sponges, cloths, and oil. "Well, that is what you asked for," I told myself aloud; and then "Thank you," louder, and was rewarded by the same feeling that Father had had: that the air was listening. I didn't like it.

By the time I had done everything I could do twice over, the sun was nearly gone; lanterns set in the doorposts of the stalls were lighting themselves. It then occurred to me that I liked the idea of going into the castle for the first time after dark even less than I had liked it a few hours ago while daylight was with me, keeping trolls and witches under cover. Greatheart had finished the grain, and was happily working on the hay hanging in a net; he was not inclined to be sympathetic to my fidgets. I patted him for the last time and went reluctantly out. The horse was calm and relaxed again, as he had always been at home until the last few days. I tried to tell myself that this was a good omen, but I felt more as if I were being betrayed in my last extremity. I closed the stable door—or anyway my hand was on it when it closed itself—on the sound of quiet chewing. I found myself twisting the griffin ring on my finger as I stepped down from the threshold.

As I stepped outside, the lanterns in the garden were

lighting up; there was a warm sweet smell of perfumed lamp oil. The silence was unbroken but for the clear tinkling of the little streams, and the slow scuff of my booted feet; there was still no sign of any living thing. I felt very small and shabby amid all this magnificence; riding Greatheart lent its own dignity, for he shone through his battered harness. The size and grandness of his new environment suited him; he might have been coming home after exile among the savages. But there was nothing grand about a small plain girl, poorly dressed, self-conscious, and jittery. I looked around me, blinking, and then turned back towards the castle. The courtyard was dark as I turned; but it leaped into a blaze of light as I looked towards it. The silver arch around the enormous front doors glittered and gleamed, and the figures molded on it seemed to come to life: a king's hunting party, the horses' manes flying, and banners and pennoncels bucking in the wind. There were hounds scattered, tails high, before the galloping horses, and two or three riders carried hooded falcons on their wrists. There were several ladies riding sidesaddle, their skirts mixing with the trailing saddleskirts. In front of the field the king rode, leaning forwards over his horse's neck; he wore a thin circlet around his forehead, his sleeves and collar were trimmed with fur, and his horse was the largest and finest. I found myself trying to read his face, and could not. He was galloping towards a great wood that stood at the peak of the arch, branches bowed like the petals of a flower. On the other side of the arch the scene was a mirror image of the first, but the story told was changed. The king's horse was plunging wildly away from the forest, riderless, its eyes rolling. The other hunters were reining back hard at the forest's edge, with expressions of shock, dismay, and dawning horror on their faces. The dogs were fleeing, tails between legs and ears flat, and the falcons struggled to be free, wings spread, claws tearing at tasseled hoods. Both scenes were colorless, icy pale, yet sharp and vigorous; I expected to see the next hoof hit the ground as I looked at a galloping horse, to see the lady's raised hand brush the scarf from her eyes; and I looked with nervous fascination at the wood, but saw nothing but the silver trees.

I saw this very clearly, but all in the space of a moment. The doors swung silently but ponderously open, revealing a great hall lit by hundreds of candles in crystal sconces. As I stood dumb and staring, a little singing breeze swept out through the doors and curled around me. I could almost hear voices in it, but when I tried to listen I lost them. It was a very small wind, and it seemed to exist only for the purpose of tugging at my sleeves and twitching the hem of my divided riding skirt, and uttering what sounded like little cries of dismay at the condition of my hair and my boots. No candle flame shivered in a draft, and no leaves tapped one against another. The breeze circled eagerly around my shoulders, and feeling that I was being encouraged, I took a few steps forwards, towards the enormous doors. I wondered how King Cophetua's beggar-maid had felt when the palace gates had first opened for her. But there was little resemblance between us; she had a king in love with her, because of her innate nobility, and a beauty that sparkled even through her rags. So much for comparisons. I went inside.

The breeze giggled and chirped at me as if I were a reluctant horse, and then dashed off before me into the hall. As I crossed the threshold a door swung open, to my right, about fifty feet down the broad front corridor. The clicking of my boot-heels had as much effect on that massive silence as the sweep of a butterfly's wings might. I went through the open door. This was a dining hall, big enough to be two ballrooms; there were three fire-places, with windows on the fourth wall that were each three times as tall as I was, and a many-legged rectangular table that might take half an hour to walk around, but only ten minutes to walk across. I looked up. There was a musicians' gallery at one end of the room, with heavy dark velvet drapes drawn across it. Its balcony was built where the second storey should have been; the ceilings were very high. I tipped my head farther back, squinting: There seemed to be a design, painted or sculptured, on the ceiling, but the candles were set no higher than the foot of the musicians' gallery, and their light did not reach so far.

I returned my gaze to the table. I saw now that it was crowded with covered dishes, silver and gold. Bottles of wine stood in buckets full of gleaming crushed ice; a bowl big enough to be a hip bath stood on a pedestal two feet tall, in the shape of Atlas bearing the world on his shoulders; and the hollow globe was full of shining fresh fruit. A hundred delightful odours assailed me. At the head of the table, near the door I had entered by, stood a huge wooden chair, carved and gilded and lined with chestnut-brown brocade over straw-colored satin. The garnet-set peak was as tall as a schooner's mast. It could have been a throne. As I looked, it slid away slightly from the table and turned itself towards me, as another chair had beckoned to my father. I noticed for the first time that it was the only chair at that great table, and there was only one place laid, although the table gleamed to its farther end with the curved backs of plate covers, and with goblets and tureens and tall jeweled pitchers.

"Good heavens, no," I said. "I can't sit there. And who's to eat all this? I can't," I said, and thought nervously, I hope it's not required. The Beast must mean to eat me after all, and means to fatten me well first. He certainly doesn't lack for food, my thoughts continued ruefully: Is his palate really so jaded that with all of this he wants young maiden too? Besides, all of this fancy stuff will probably disagree with me.

At once my breeze was back, *tsk-tsk*ing and scolding and banging at the backs of my knees and all but dragging me to where the great chair waited in lofty silence. I sat on it timidly, feeling smaller and more bedraggled than ever, and much the worse for the day's dirt. A white linen napkin unfolded itself and blew onto my patched homespun lap. There were seven spoons and seven forks, four knives and five goblets of different shapes and colors lined up before me. A little table walked out of nowhere to my left elbow, bearing hot water and soap and thick towels; while I was occupied with these, dishes were jingling merrily back and forth across the table, and I turned back to a plate heaped high with delicacies.

The tentative thoughts I had entertained about refusing to eat and thus spoiling the Beast's plans for me melted away at once like butter in a hot skillet. The knowledge that I had eaten nothing since breakfast, and that twelve hours ago, reasserted itself forcefully, and I made an excellent dinner. I recognized very few of the dishes I was offered, but everything I sampled was superb. I was soon bemused by a variety that surpassed anything I had known at the finest banquets in the city. It was after I was finished, leaning back with a sigh, that my fears rushed back to me, as if they had only been waiting till I was revived enough to pay them proper attention. I stood up abruptly without another thought for that wonderful table, and walked to the door. I wouldn't wait any longer; I must know tonight what my doom was to be. If the Beast would not come to me, very well then, I would look for him.

Dinner had refreshed me, and I set out if not eagerly at least energetically. I walked across more corridors, up and down more stairs, and in and out of more rooms than I cared to count. I saw furniture and whatnots in all the styles and designs I had ever seen or heard of, plus many more that were entirely outside my experience. There were tables and chairs and divans in black wood, and in all the hues of brown; in ivory and alabaster and bone; even in brass and copper and jade, silver and gold. I saw no sign of anything less than the finest of craftsmanship. There were tapestries on the walls, and hundreds of paintings, mostly sea- and landscapes; very few people figured in any of the scenes, and few animals. There were no hunting scenes of any sort, nor any souvenirs of the chase, antlers or stuffed trophies or weapons, hung on the walls. There was statuary on elegant pedestals, or standing in alcoves; china displayed in cabinets; gorgeous rugs alternated with polished floors of marble or inlaid wood. There were no clocks and no mirrors.

I soon lost my sense of direction, and then most of my sense of purpose, but I kept walking. The fine dinner, the strange new surroundings, and my apprehensions combined to keep me feeling alert and wide awake. But I found that the beauties of the castle began to blur before my eyes; there was too much to take in, as there had been in the garden during the afternoon, and more recently in the dining hall.

After a while, perhaps hours, I came to a door at the end of a corridor, just around a corner; on this door was a golden plaque. As I approached, the candelabra set in two niches on each side of the door lit themselves—I was becoming accustomed to being preceded in my wanderings by invisible pages carrying invisible tinder, which never sputtered and always lit the first time—and on the plaque I read: "Beauty's Room." I just had time enough to make out the words before the door opened inwards.

I hesitated. It might be my name, of course, but then it was also possible that the plaque had something a little more abstract in mind, and if I crossed the threshold I should be blasted at once. On the other hand, I had no idea of the rules of the game I was now playing; and if the castle or its owner was trying to trap me, there were easier ways. That I was here at all was a gesture of defeat and surrender. I looked inside. It was a room for a princess, even in this castle full of wonders: An enormous bed stood on a dais, canopied in gold, with a white counterpane worked in scarlet and green. Tall wardrobes stood back against the wall to one side of the bed, and as I looked at them their doors burst open as if from the pressure of the hundreds of beautiful gowns that hung inside. A bolt of deep-blue silk stitched with silver thread in the shapes of flying birds fell from some hidden shelf at the top of one wardrobe and unrolled itself almost to my feet, across the amber-figured carpet. Beside the wardrobes were low tables, and upon them were placed jewelry boxes as rare and beautiful as the jewels they contained, and more brushes and combs than a dozen vain princesses could use. There were cut-crystal bottles of perfume with emerald caps, and vases full of red and white roses; their perfume shimmered in the air like a rainbow.

On the other side of the room was an arched wall of windows that reached, in rows and rows of tiny panes, from the high ceiling to the padded gold-and-white-velvet window seat. Then with a small gasp I stepped into the room, philosophical questions on the nature of Beauty forgotten, because the walls that met the window on each side were lined with bookshelves. There were hundreds of leather-bound volumes, regal and wise. My fingers touched the smooth bindings reverently. There was a desk with enough drawers and pigeonholes for the most—or least—organized of scholars, a tall pile of fine white paper, a dozen colors of ink in gilt or cut-glass bottles, and pens and nibs by the hundreds. I sat down at the desk and stared at it all.

Then my breeze came back, as if I had had more than enough time to riffle through smooth paper and line up the pens in rows. It whisked under my fingers and around my chair, and drew my attention to the fireplace behind me, opposite the bed, and the deep ivory-and-silver-colored bathtub drawn up near it. The tub was receiving its last jugful of steaming perfumed water as I watched—floating china jugs were more disturbing than invisible pages, I decided—and towels curled over the back of an armchair. There was no reason why the victim shouldn't present herself for her doom after she was properly washed; and it would doubtless be good for morale.

It was. And the enchanted soap didn't get in my eyes. The breeze, which had been tossing about washcloths and back-brushes and towels, combed my hair and strung a jade-green ribbon through it, and then presented me with a pale-green dress with yards and yards of frothy billowing skirt sewn all over with tiny winking diamonds. "Ha," I said. "I will wear nothing of the kind."

The breeze and I had quite a little struggle after that over what I would put on—my old clothes had disappeared while I bathed—by the end of which my hair had escaped its ribbon, and the breeze was racing around the room whistling angrily to itself. It sizzled through the long silk fringe of the canopy and hurled to the length of their twisted cords the heavy golden tassels that tied back the bed-curtains. There were dresses scattered all over the floor and across the bed and backs of chairs in gorgeous colored heaps. And I still wasn't happy about what I finally did agree to wear: It was much simpler than the green dress, but there were still pearls on the white bodice, and the skirt was golden velvet, a few shades paler than the canopy.

I turned towards the door again at last. It must be very late, but I still felt that I couldn't sleep until I knew what was going to happen to me—even if thus seeking it out was only hastening the end. I left "Beauty's Room" and stood for a moment in the hall, watching the bright plaque catch fire and shadow in the candlelight as the door shut behind me. I turned away to walk more corridors, more tall arched and pillared rooms. I spent little time looking at the wonders I passed; I was too intent on that one thing: finding my host, or my gaoler. I paused at last on a balcony over-looking a large dim hall similar to the one I had eaten dinner in. Candles lit themselves only a few feet ahead of me as I walked, and beyond them all was darkness; after I had passed, in a minute or two, they winked out again, as I saw when I turned once or twice to watch them. The big windows, when they were not muffled with curtains, showed only as paler grey shapes in the walls; there was no moon yet to shine through them. But then, looking up again, I thought I saw a golden edge of light to a partly open door, beyond the glow of my entourage of lighted candles. My heart began to beat very much faster, and I made my way quietly towards that door.

Like all of the other doors I had met in the castle, this one opened at my approach. A few days of this and I would forget the operation of a latch or a door-handle. The room it revealed was a large, warm, and gracious one, although small by the standards of this castle. On one wall to my left a fire was burning in a fireplace framed with wrought iron in the shape of climbing vines; two armchairs were drawn up before it. One chair was empty. In the other a massive shadow sat. Except for the faint and flickering light of the fire the room was in darkness; there was a table behind the occupied armchair, and on it stood a candelabrum of a dozen tall candles, but they remained dark. I realized I was standing in a little halo of light, the candles in the hall shining around me as I stood on the threshold. My eyes slowly adjusted themselves to the gloom beyond the door. I caught a gleam of dark-green velvet on what might have been a knee in the shadowed armchair. "Good evening, Beauty," said a great harsh voice.

I shivered, and put a hand to the door-frame, and tried to take courage from the fact that the Beast—for it must be he—had not devoured me at once. "Good evening, milord," I said. My voice was misleadingly steady.

"I am the Beast," was the reply. "You will call me that, please." A pause. "Have you come of your own free will to stay in my castle?"

"I have," I said, as bravely as I could.

"Then I am much obliged to you." This was said in so quiet a voice, notwithstanding the deep rumbling echo that was part of every word, and was so totally different a greeting from what I was expecting that I was shocked into saying before I thought:

"Obliged! Milord, you gave me no choice. I could not let my father die for the sake of a silly rose."

"Do you hate me then?" The rough voice sounded almost wistful.

Again I was taken aback. "Well, you give me little cause to love you." I thought then guiltily of the fine meal, and the beautiful room—especially the books. It occurred to me for the first time that if he had planned to eat me immediately it was unlikely, or at least curious, that he should have provided me with enough books for years' reading.

The immense shadow shifted in its chair. I was sure of the knee, now, and the velvet; and now I could see a glitter of eyes, and also—perhaps—of sharp claws. I looked hastily away from the claws. The feet were lost in the pool of darkness beneath the wrought-iron grate.

"Would it help perhaps if I told you that, had your father returned to me alone, I would have sent him on his way unharmed?"

"You *would?*" I said; it was half a shriek. "You mean that I came here for nothing?"

A shadowy movement like the shaking of a great shaggy head. "No. Not what you would count as nothing. He would have returned to you, and you would have been glad, but you also would have been ashamed, because you had sent him, as you thought, to his death. Your shame would have grown until you came to hate the sight of your father, because he reminded you of a deed you hated, and hated yourself for. In time it would have ruined your peace and happiness, and at last your mind and heart."

My tired brain refused to follow this. "But—I could not have let him go alone," I said, bewildered.

"Yes," said the Beast.

I thought about it for a minute. "Can you see the future, then?" I asked uneasily.

"Not exactly," said the shadow. "But I can see you."

There didn't seem to be any answer to that, either. "I cannot see you at all, milord," I ventured timidly.

Again the gleam of eyes. "Indeed," said the Beast. "I should have welcomed you when you first arrived this afternoon; but I thought candlelight might be a little kinder for a first impression of such as me." He stood up, straightening himself slowly, but I still shrank back. He must have been seven feet tall at full height, with proportionate breadth of shoulder and chest, like the great black bears of the north woods that could break a hunter's back with one blow of a heavy paw. He stood still for a moment, as if waiting for me to recover myself, and then with a sigh as deep as a storm wind, he raised the candelabrum from the table. It lit as he brought it to shoulder level, and I was staring suddenly into his face. "Oh no," I cried, and covered my own face with my hands. But when I heard him take a step towards me, I leaped back in alarm like a deer at the crack of a branch nearby, turning my eyes away from him.

"You have nothing to fear," the Beast said, as gently as his harsh voice allowed.

After a moment I looked up again. He was still standing, watching me with those eyes. I realized that what made his gaze so awful was that his eyes were human. We looked at each other a moment. Not bearish at all, I decided. Not like anything else I could put a name to either. If Yggdrasil had been given an animal's shape, it might have looked like the Beast.

"Forgive me," he said, "but I am somewhat shortsighted, and I would like a closer look at you." He stepped forwards again, and I backed up until I reached the balcony. I wrapped my fingers around the railing and stood: cornered, with the hunter's lantern shining in my eyes. "You—you aren't going to—eat me?" I quavered.

He stopped as if he had walked into a tree, and the candlestick in his hand dropped several inches. "*Eat you?*" he said, with convincing horror. "Certainly not. What made you think so? Have you not been well looked after since you arrived? Have I frightened you—in any fashion that I could avoid?"

"I—Well, I couldn't think of any other reason for your—er—inviting me here."

"Did I not tell your father that no harm should come to his daughter?" I opened my mouth, and then shut it again, and he continued sadly: "No, you need say nothing. I am a Beast, and a Beast has no honour. But you may trust my word: You are safe here, in my castle and anywhere on my lands."

My curiosity, at least for the moment, was stronger than fear or courtesy; his gentle mien encouraged me, and I need not look into his face; I would look no higher than his waistcoat buttons, which were about at my eye level anyway. "Then why?"

"Well—I lack companionship. It is rather lonesome here sometimes, with no one to talk to," he said simply.

My sudden sympathy must have shown on my face, for he raised the light again, and as he came closer I looked up at him with very little fear, although I still leaned against the balustrade. But he looked at me so long that I became uneasy again. I couldn't read his expression; the face was too unlike any I was accustomed to. "I—er—I hope you weren't misled by my foolish nickname," I said. What if he was angry at being cheated of Beauty, and killed me for tricking him?

"Misled?" he said. "No. I think your name suits you very well."

"Oh *no*," I said. It was my turn for the tone of convincing horror. "I assure you I am *very* plain."

"Are you?" he said, musingly. He turned away, and

set the candelabrum in a conveniently unoccupied niche in the tapestry-hung wall. The hall was lit as brightly as a ballroom although the room we had just left was still dim and rosy with firelight. "I have been out of the world a long time, of course, but I do not believe I am so shortsighted as all that."

I was not used to being struck dumb more than once in a conversation. I must be more tired and overwrought than I thought.

"You say that Beauty is your nickname?" he said after a moment. "What is your given name then?"

"Honour," I said.

Something that might have been a smile exposed too many long white teeth. "I welcome Beauty and Honour both, then," he said. "Indeed, I am very fortunate."

Oh dear, I thought. Then my mind went back to something he had said earlier: "If you wanted someone to talk to," I said, "why didn't you keep my father? He knows many more interesting things than I do."

"Mmm," said the Beast. "I'm afraid I specifically wanted a girl."

"Oh?" I said nervously. "Why?"

He turned away from me, walked back to the doorway, and stood, head bowed, hands clasped behind him. The silence squeezed at my heart. "I am looking for a wife," he said, heavily. "Will you marry me, Beauty?"

My fear, which I had had mostly under control, boiled up again and became panic. "Oh!" I said. "What shall I say?"

"Answer yes or no without fear," said the Beast without raising his head.

"Oh no, Beast," I cried. I wanted to run away, but I thought of him chasing after me, and I stayed where I was.

There was a long stricken pause. "Very well," he said at last. "I will bid you good night. Sleep easily, Beauty: Remember, you have nothing to fear."

I didn't move. "Well, go on," he said gruffly, with a wave of one arm. "I know you are longing to escape. I shan't follow you." He walked into his room, and the door began to close.

"Good night," I called. The door paused a moment, and then shut with a soft click. I turned and ran, back down the corridor the way I had come.

The life I had lived over the last years enabled me to run a long time. I didn't look where I was going, I simply ran in the direction that my fear told me was "away." My soft shoes were as light as leaves and made almost no sound, but the long heavy skirt slowed me down. I stopped at last, gasping for breath; my rationality slowly reasserted itself, and I realized with dismay that, once again, I was lost. I took a few steps forwards and looked around a corner: And there was "Beauty's Room." The door opened at once and a faint smell of lavender curled around me. I was sure the room had been at the end of a long corridor before—of course, it was easy to mistake things by candlelight—but no matter.

I went inside, exhausted and grateful, and collapsed on the bed. The smell of lavender came from the fresh white sheets; the bedclothes were folded back invitingly. The breeze, which seemed to have been toasting its toes by the fire and waiting up for me, whisked over to help me undress, tutting over my wind-blown hair and rumpled skirts. My hair was combed out and braided expertly, and I was swept into a long white nightgown of the softest silk with ivory-colored roses embroidered on it. I climbed into the big bed and was tucked up; the candles blew out, with a most un-candle-like smell of cinnamon, and the fire burned low and banked itself.

But I couldn't sleep. I tossed and turned until I had pulled the sheets and blankets all awry, and lost one pillow on the floor; rather to my surprise, when I discovered its loss, it showed no sign of replacing itself. I lay still for a few minutes, staring at the canopy arched over me: From where I lay looking up, the picture was of a griffin, head thrown back, claws and wings extended, and spiked tail lashing around its hind feet. It reminded me of my ring; I had taken it off while I bathed, and hadn't replaced it. This was as good an excuse as any. I slid out of the ravaged bed and down the three steps to floor level. The ring lay, glittering faintly, on a little table by the fire. I picked it up, looked at it for a minute, put it on.

I wasn't ready to go back to bed. I noticed, glancing in its direction, that it was busy setting itself to rights; it would be only polite to leave it alone for a little while. I wandered restlessly around the room and paused beside the bookshelves; but I didn't feel like reading. I curled up finally on the window seat and looked out, leaning my forehead against the cool glass. The moon, now risen high above the horizon, was nearly full; it shed silver on the broad fields, and the black forest beyond, on the gardens and ornamental trees; even on the tall grim tower that reached out on my left towards the tall grim forest far across the meadows. The lanterns in the garden were dark. As I tried to look at the scene more closely there seemed to be a curious patchy darkness that skittered across the landscape. There were clouds in the sky to be sure, but they moved slowly, not with the restless elusive swiftness of this pattern of shadow; and the moon shone undisturbed. I blinked, rubbed my eyes; they must be playing tricks on me. And I thought: This whole castle is like one dreadful joke—in spite of the hospitable efforts of food that serves itself, hot water that pours itself, candles that blink themselves on and off. Event the friendly breeze had left me, the nearest thing to a living presence I had met—except the Beast. "Have no fear," he had said.

The silence was complete; even ashes from the fire fell without sound. I shivered, tapped a finger against the glass, just to make a noise. "This will never do," I said aloud. *Have no fear, have no fear, have no fear. You may trust my word: You are safe here, in my castle and anywhere on my lands* hissed like winter wind in my mind.

Greatheart, I thought. I will go visit him. That will calm me down, to stroke his warm cheek and have him rest his heavy head on my shoulder. I used to take naps in the stable with the carriage horses when I was a baby; I still found stables and their occupants very soothing in times of stress.

I slid off the window seat and walked to the door; but it didn't open. Surprised, I put my hand to it; there was no response. I seized the handle in both hands and pulled at it with all my strength; it was as though it were part of the wall. It didn't even rattle on a lock or a hinge; in the rising tide of panic in my mind, thoughts floated: It was solid, this door had never opened, it would never open. I screamed, "No—let me out, please let me out!" and pounded the silent panels with my fists, till the skin broke and bled. I sank to my knees at last, weeping, and tucked my poor aching hands under my arms. I sobbed, my forehead pressed against the unyielding door, till the calm of utter exhaustion took me. I stumbled back to bed.

At the edge of sleep it seemed that the breeze returned, and something cool was put on my hands so that the pain slipped away like a thief in shadow. The gentle whistling and sighing of the breeze resolved itself at last into words, but I was too near sleep to hear much of what was said, or to be certain that I was not listening to a dream. There were two voices. The first said: "Poor child, poor child. I feel for her sadly. If only there were some way we could help her."

The second voice said, "But there isn't, dear. You

know that. We do our best; but she must find her own way."

"I know. But it seems so hard."

"It does, and it is; but cheer up. She is a good girl, and he loves her already. It will be all right in time. . . ."

⚕ 2 ⚕

When I woke up the sun was high in the sky, staining the dark-red carpet with long rectangles of light, turning the amber pattern the color of pale honey. In the first moment of consciousness, when I knew it was very late but before I opened my eyes, I thought, "How can I have slept so late? I'll never get all my work done. Why didn't they wake me?" And then I remembered, and I opened my eyes, and recognized the feel of fine linen under my cheek and fingers; and as memory returned, I realized what it was that had awakened me: the delicious, insidious smells of hot chocolate and of buttered toast. I sat up. Breakfast was laid on the table by the fire, which was burning once again. I bounced joyfully out of bed. Every morning in the city my maid had brought me toast and chocolate: How did they know? As I swung my feet to the floor, I pressed the mattress firmly with my hands, and was rewarded with sharp twists of pain. I sobered, looking down at my hands, thinking of the night before. They had been wrapped in gauze while I slept; perhaps that had something to do with the odd conversation I thought I'd heard, just before sleep claimed me. I frowned, trying to remember precisely; but I soon gave it up, the hot chocolate being much more interesting. There were also oranges and apples in a golden bowl, and a little ebony-handled knife for peeling.

The breeze arrived when I was finished, to whisk everything away by bundling it up in the linen tablecloth and making it vanish in midair; and after some grumbling on both sides it and I settled on a morning dress of grey, with silver buttons, and elegant black boots with braided laces. I had been avoiding looking at the door; but when at last I uneasily approached it, it swung open without hesitation. I ran out, as if it might change its mind; the breeze swirled once around me and left.

The castle looked very different with bright sunshine flooding through the tall windows; the sombre magnificence I had seen last night by candle- and lamp-light was lit up to a rich but cheerful splendour. It was even hard to believe in the Beast; he seemed a creature from a bad dream, and no part of this handsome palace. In this mood, I refused to consider why it was that I was here at all, and I set myself to admiring my surroundings without thinking about it. I found my way to some stairs to descend, and shortly to the great front hall with the dining room opening off it, and out through the huge front doors.

Greatheart was glad to see me. He put his head over the stall door and neighed like thunder when he heard my step. "I don't blame you—I've been lonesome too," I said. "Let's explore a bit together." I snapped a lead rope, which I found by turning round and looking for it, onto his halter and led him out into the sun. He shook his mane and stamped his feet and expressed general approval; and we wandered through the gorgeous gardens, looking at the flowers and the statuary. There were roses everywhere among hundreds of other kinds of flowers, but I did not see any rose arbour like the one Father had described. Greatheart blew at the flowers, but like a well-bred horse, he offered to eat nothing but the grass; this he tore up in mouthfuls. We found a patch of clover by and by, and paused there awhile for him to graze in earnest. "You will get as round as a broodmare, at this rate," I told him. "I will take you for a good hard ride—after *my* lunch." I took him back to his stable, and went inside the castle; but when the dining-hall door began to open, I called, "I'd really rather eat in my room, if you don't mind," it paused, and then closed again, reluctantly; and I found an excellent lunch laid on the little table in "Beauty's Room."

"The only problem with this place is the silence," I said conversationally to my teacup. "Even the fire burns quietly; and while I can't fault the service"—and I wondered if there were anything to hear—"I could almost like a little more rattling of cutlery and so forth. It makes a house, or even a castle, seem lived-in." I took my teacup over to the window. "I've never liked house pets much—monkeys are a nuisance, dogs shed and make me sneeze, and cats claw things—but birds, now. It would be very nice to have Orpheus here to sing to me." I found a latch to the window, and a section of it swung out, noiselessly of course. "Not even any birds here," I continued, leaning out. "I can see how anything that goes on feet would want to stay out of his way; but surely he doesn't control the sky." There was a broad window ledge with a shallow flat-bottomed trench cut into it. "Just the thing for birds," I said, and found a tin at my elbow, with jeweled peacocks painted on it, full of mixed seeds such as a bird might like. I spread several generous handfuls of this along the ledge. "All I ask is a few sparrows," I said. "The only peacocks I ever knew bit people."

I looked out across the gardens. It was odd that no birds had found those trees and flowers. "Perhaps they're only waiting to be asked," I said. "Well, consider yourself invited," I said loudly. "On my behalf, anyway." I closed the window again, changed into a divided skirt more or less suitable for riding—"Haven't you ever heard of *plain* clothing?" I said in exasperation, searching through the wardrobes for a blouse without ribbons or jewels or lace, while the breeze plucked protestingly at my elbows—and went out again to take Greatheart for his ride.

He was feeling lively, and once we were beyond the stately gardens with their trim paths it took very little urging to get him into his long-striding gallop. The air was cold, out beyond the gardens; I had brought a cloak, and after pulling Greatheart down to a jog, I wrapped it around me. I had expected to reach the tall holly hedge that bounded my prison fairly soon; it had not taken so very long to ride in the night before, and Father had seen the gates from the garden. But now we walked and trotted through fields, and stands of trees, and more fields, and more trees. It was wilder country here, with rocks and twisted scrub, and the ground underfoot was uneven. I wondered if perhaps the hedge did not extend all the way around the Beast's lands, and perhaps we had re-entered the fringes of the enchanted forest. Not that that would be very useful, I thought; I'd probably just find that carriage-road again, and be led straight back. And I don't fancy trying to find my way out till I starve to death.

There were even patches of snow where we were walking. I turned to look over my shoulder. I could still see the castle towers dark and solemn against the clear blue sky, but they were getting far away. "Time we were heading back," I said, reined him round, and kneed him into a ponderous canter. "Back home, I suppose," I said thoughtfully. It wouldn't do to try to escape on my very first day anyway, I thought. Particularly since it wouldn't do any good.

The sun was low in the sky by the time I had stabled Greatheart, groomed him, and again cleaned the tack by hand. "Yes, and I did notice that all the mended bits have been replaced, and I thank you," I said aloud, polishing the bits. If I didn't do it, the invisible hands would; I had also noticed that the bits and buckles had been shined to mirror hue after I'd left them a respectable glossy clean last night, and felt that I was being put on my mettle. My hands were still bandaged; they felt a little stiff, but they no longer troubled me—and the magic bandages didn't get soiled, even after I'd soaped and oiled the leather.

I went a little way into the garden after leaving the stable and sat on a marble bench, still warm from the sun, to watch the afternoon change to evening grey and flame. Or at any rate it could be the sun that warmed it, I thought; I also took notice that the bench was just the right height for someone of my short length of leg. I turned my head to look over another sweep of the gardens, and saw the Beast coming towards me. He was already very near, and I bit back a cry; he walked as silently as the shadows crawling towards my feet, in spite of the heavy boots he wore. Today he was wearing brown velvet, the color of cloves, and there was ivory-colored lace at his throat, and hanging low over the backs of his hands.

"Good evening, Beauty," he said.

"Good evening, Beast," I replied, and stood up.

"Please don't let me disturb you," he said humbly. "I will go away again if you prefer."

"Oh no," I said hastily, trying to be polite. "Will you walk a little? I love to see the sun set over a garden, and yours are so fine." We walked in silence for a minute or two; I've had better ideas, I thought, taking three steps to his one, although I could see that he was adjusting his pace to mine as best he could. Presently I said, a little out of breath, but finding the silence uncomfortable: "Sunset was my favorite time of the day when we lived in the city; I used to walk in our garden there, but the walls were too high. When the sky was most beautiful, our garden was already dark."

"Sunset no longer pleases you?" the Beast inquired, as one who will do his duty by the conversation.

"I'd never seen a sunrise—I was always asleep," I explained. "I used to stay up very late, reading. Then we moved to the country—I suppose I like sunrise best now; I'm too tired, usually, by sunset, to appreciate it, and I'm usually in a hurry to finish something and go in to supper—or I was," I said sadly. Longing for home broke over me suddenly and awfully, and closed my throat.

We came to a wall covered with climbing roses which I recognized at once: This must be where Father had met the Beast. We went through the break in the wall, and I looked around me at the glorious confusion; the Beast halted a few steps behind me. Then suddenly in a final fierce bloom of light before it disappeared, the sun filled the castle and its gardens with gold, like nectar in a crystal goblet; the roses gleamed like facets. We both turned towards the light, and I found myself gazing at the back of the Beast's head. I saw that the heavy brown mane that fell to his shoulders was streaked with grey. The light went out like a snuffed candle, and we stood in soft grey twilight; the sky the sun had left behind was pink and lavender.

The Beast turned back to me. I could look at him fairly steadily this time. After a moment he said harshly: "I am very ugly, am I not?"

"You are certainly, uh, very hairy," I said.

"You are being polite," he said.

"Well, yes," I conceded. "But then you called me beautiful, last night."

He made a noise somewhere between a roar and a bark, and after an anxious minute, I decided it was probably a laugh. "You do not believe me then?" he inquired.

"Well—no," I said, hesitantly, wondering if this might anger him. "Any number of mirrors have told me otherwise."

"You will find no mirrors here," he said, "for I cannot bear them: nor any quiet water in ponds. And since I am the only one who sees you, why are you not then beautiful?"

"But—" I said, and Platonic principles rushed into my mouth so fast that they choked me silent. After a moment's reflection I decided against a treatise on the absolute, and I said, to say something: "There's always Greatheart. Although I've never noticed that he minds how I look."

"Greatheart?"

"My horse. The big grey stallion in your stable." '

"Ah, yes," he said, and looked at the ground.

"Is anything wrong?" I said anxiously.

"It would have been better, perhaps, if you had sent him back with your father," said the Beast.

"Oh dear—is he not safe? Oh, tell me nothing will happen to him! Could I not send him back now? I won't have him hurt," I said.

The Beast shook his head. "He's safe enough; but you see—beasts—other beasts don't like me. You've noticed that nothing lives in the garden but trees and grass and flowers, and rocks and water."

"You'll not hurt him?" I said again.

"No; but I could, and horses know it. As I recall, your father's horse would not come through my gates a second time."

"That's true," I whispered.

"There's no need to worry. You know now. You look after him well, and I will take care to stay away from him."

"Perhaps—perhaps it would be better if he went home," I said, although my heart sank at the thought of losing him. "Could you—send him?"

"I could, but not in any fashion that he would understand, and it would drive him mad. He will be all right."

I looked up at him, wanting to believe him, and found to my surprise that I did. I smiled. "All right."

"Come; it's getting dark. Shall we go in? May I join you at your dinner?"

"Of course," I said. "You are master here."

"No, Beauty; it is you who are mistress. Ask for anything I can give you, and you shall have it."

"My freedom" sat on my tongue, but I did not say it aloud.

"Is your room as you wish? Is there anything you would change?"

"No—no. Everything is perfect. You are very kind."

He brushed this away impatiently. "I don't want your thanks. Is the bed comfortable? Did you sleep well last night?"

"Yes, of course, very well," I said, but an involuntary

gesture of my hands caught his eye.

"What have you done to your hands?" he demanded.

"I—oh—" I said, and realized I could not lie to him, although I did not understand why. "Last night—I tried to go out of my room. The door wouldn't open, and—I was frightened."

"I see," he said; it was no more than a rumble deep in his chest. "It was on my orders that the door was locked."

"You said I had nothing to fear," I said.

"That is so; but I am a Beast, and I cannot always behave prettily—even for you," he replied.

"I am sorry," I said. "I did not understand." There was something about the way he stood there without looking at me: Resignation born of long silent hopeless years sat heavily on him, and I found myself involuntarily anxious to comfort him. "But I am quite recovered now in my mind—and see: I am sure my hands are nearly healed too." I pulled the bandages off as I spoke, and held my hands out for inspection. I had forgotten my ring; the diamonds and the bright ruby eyes caught a few drops of the last daylight and glittered.

"Do you like your ring?" he asked after a pause, looking at my hands.

"Yes," I said. "Very much. And thank you for the rose

seeds, too. I planted them right after Father came home, and they bloomed the day I left—so I can remember the house all covered with them," I said wistfully.

"I'm glad. I tried to hurry them along, of course, but it's rather difficult to do at a distance. "

"Is it?" I said, not sure if an answer was required; and I remembered how the vines nearest the forest had grown the fastest. "And thank you for all the lovely things in Father's saddle-bags—it was very kind of you."

"I am not kind—you know you are thinking right now that you would much rather be without rings and roses and lace tablecloths, and be home again instead—and I don't want your gratitude. I told you that already," he said roughly. After a moment he continued in a different tone: "It was difficult to know what to send. Emeralds, sapphires, the usual king's ransom and so forth, I didn't think would be much good to you. Even gold coins might be difficult to use."

"You chose very well," I said.

"Did I really?" he sounded pleased. "Or are you just being polite again?"

"No, really," I said. "I used two of the candles myself, reading. It was very extravagant of me, but it was wonderful to have good, even light to read by."

"I sent more candles this time," he said. "And furs, and cloth. I didn't want to send more money." Blood money, I thought.

"It's dark," he said. "Your dinner will be waiting. Will you take my arm?"

"I'd rather not," I said.

"Very well," he replied.

"Let's hurry," I said, looking away from him. "I'm very hungry."

The dining hall lit up at our approach. I had noticed without thinking about it that while dusk was falling as we stood in the gardens, and the pedestal lanterns were lighting elsewhere, we stood among the roses in a little pool of shadow, and the lanterns that lined our path back towards the castle remained dark.

"That's odd," I said. "Don't they usually light as you approach? The candles did, last night, when I was walking through the castle."

He made a noise like a grunt with words in it, but in no language I knew; and the lamps lit at once.

"I don't understand," I said.

He glanced at me. "I have long preferred the dark."

I could think of no response; and we entered the castle. The same immense table stood, heavily laden with fine china and crystal and silver and gold, and I recognized not one cup or bowl or plate from the night before; and the air was crowded with savory smells. The Beast stood behind the great carved chair and bowed me into it; and called another chair over to him from where it stood in a row of tall chairs, no two alike, lined up against the wall. The words he used were as unfamiliar as those he had spoken to the lamps in the garden.

Then the little table with hot water and towels trotted up to me, and while I busied myself with that, serving platters jostled and rang against each other in their haste to serve my plate. A little rattling cutlery, I thought. But here even clanks and collisions are musical—I suppose because they're made of such fine materials. What am I doing here? Grace would have looked magnificent in a throne. I feel foolish.

I glanced over at the Beast, who was sitting a little way down the table on my right. He was leaning back in his chair with one velvet knee against the table, and no place laid for him.

"Are you not joining me?" I asked in surprise.

He raised his hands—or paws, or claws. "I am a Beast," he said. "I cannot wield knife and fork. Would you rather I left you?"

"No," I said, and this time I didn't need to remember to be polite. "No; it's nice to have company. It is lonesome here—the silence presses around so."

"Yes, I know," he said, and I thought of what he had said the previous night. "Beauty," he said, watching the parade past my plate, "you shouldn't let them bully you that way. You can have anything you would like to eat; you need only ask for it."

"Everything looks and smells so delicious, I couldn't choose. I don't mind having the decision taken out of my hands." Around a mouthful I said: "You say I need only ask—yet the words I've heard you say, to the lanterns outside, and your chair here, are no language I recognize."

"Yes; when enchantments are dragged from their world into ours they tend to be rather slow and grudging about learning the local language. But I've assigned two—er—well, call them handmaids, to you that should understand you."

"The little breeze that chatters at me," I said.

"Yes; they should seem a little more real—almost substantial to you. They're very near our world."

I chewed thoughtfully. "You talk as if this were all very obvious, but I don't understand at all."

"I'm sorry," he said. "It is rather complicated; I've

had a long time to accustom myself to the arrangements here, but little practice in explaining them to an outsider."

I looked again at the grey in his hair. "You are not a very—young Beast, are you?" I said.

"No," he answered, and paused. "I have been here about two hundred years, I think."

He did not give me time to recover from this, but went on as I stared at him, stunned, thinking, two centuries!

"Have you had any difficulty making your wants known? I will gladly assist you if necessary."

"No-o," I said, dragging myself back to the present. "But how would I find you if I needed you?"

"I am easily found," he said, "if you want me." Shortly after that I finished my meal, and stood up. "I will wish you good night now, milord," I said. "I find that I am already tired."

Sitting in his chair, he was nearly as tall as my standing height. "Beauty, will you marry me?" he said.

I took a step backwards. "No," I said.

"Do not be afraid," he said, but he sounded unhappy. "Good night, Beauty."

I went directly to bed and slept soundly. I heard no strange voices and felt no fear.

• • •

Several weeks passed, more quickly than I would have believed possible during those first few days. My time fell into a sort of schedule. I rose early in the morning, and after breakfast in my room went out into the gardens for a walk. I usually took Greatheart with me, on his lead rope. At home he used to follow me around like a pet dog, and sometimes when I was working in the shop for an afternoon I would let him loose to graze in the meadow that surrounded our house. He would wander over to the shop occasionally, and fill up the doorway with his shoulders while he watched Ger and me for a few minutes before returning to his meanderings. Since the Beast had warned me about other animals' dislike of him, I had thought it wise to keep a lead on my big horse, though in fact if he had ever taken it into his head to bolt, my small strength would not have been able to do much about it. But the Beast stayed away from us, and I never saw Greatheart exhibit any uneasiness; he was placid to the point of sleepiness, and as sweet-natured as ever. Ger had been right; having him with me in exile made a big difference in my courage.

About mid-morning I returned to the castle and spent the hours till lunch reading and studying. I had forgotten more of my Greek and Latin in the nearly three years

I'd been away from them than I liked to admit; and my French, which had always been weak, had been reduced to near nonexistence. One day, in a temper at my own stupidity, I was prowling through the bookshelves for something to relax me, and found a complete *Faerie Queen*. I had only had the opportunity to read the first two cantos before, and I seized upon these volumes with delight.

After lunch, I read again; usually *Faerie Queen* or *Le Morte d'Artbur,* after studying languages all morning, until mid-afternoon, when I changed into riding clothes and went out to take Greatheart for a gallop. Nearly every day we found ourselves traveling over unfamiliar ground, even when I thought I was deliberately choosing a route we had previously traced; even when I thought I recognized a particular group of trees or flower-strewn meadow, I could not be sure of it. I didn't know whether this was caused by the fact that my sense of direction was worse than I'd realized, which was certainly possible, or whether the paths and fields really changed from day to day—which I thought was also possible. One afternoon we rode out farther than usual, while I was preoccupied with going over the morning's reading in my mind. I realized with dismay that the sun was almost down when we finally turned back. I didn't like the idea of trying to find our way after dark—or rather, I did not like the idea of being abroad on this haunted estate after the sun set—but by some sympathetic magic less than an hour's steady jog-trot and canter brought us to the garden borders. I was sure we had been nearly three hours riding out.

But usually I had Greatheart stabled, groomed, and fed before the light faded, so that I could watch the sun set from the gardens, as I had truthfully told the Beast I liked to do. He usually met me then, in the gardens, and we walked together—I learned to trot along beside him without being too obvious about how difficult I found him to keep up with—and sometimes talked, and sometimes didn't, and watched the sky turn colors. When it had paled to mauve or dusty gold, we went inside and he sat with me in the great dining hall while I ate my dinner.

After the first few days of my enforced visit I had adopted the habit of going upstairs first, to dress for dinner. This had been one of the civilized niceties I was most pleased to dispense with after my family had left the city; but the magnificence of the Beast's dining hall cowed me. At least I could make a few of the right gestures, even if I did look more like the scullery-maid caught trying on her mistress's clothes than the gracious lady herself.

After dinner I went back to my room and read for a few more hours beside the fire before going to bed. And every night after dinner at the moment of parting, the Beast said: "Will you marry me, Beauty?" And every night I said, "No," and a little tremor of fear ran through me. As I came to know him better, the fear changed to pity, and then, almost, to sorrow; but I could not marry him, however much I came to dislike hurting him.

I never went outside after dark. We came in to dinner as soon as the sun sank and took its brilliant colors with it. When I had retired to my room after dinner I did not leave it again, and carefully avoided trying the door—or even going near it; nor did I look from my window into the gardens after the lanterns extinguished themselves at about midnight.

I missed my family terribly, and the pain of losing them eased very little as the weeks passed, but I learned to live with it, or around it. To my surprise, I also learned to be cautiously happy in my new life. In our life in the city my two greatest passions had been for books and horseback riding, and here I had as much as I wanted of each. I also had one other thing I valued highly, although my generally unsocial nature had never before been forced to admit it: companionship. I liked and needed solitude, for study and reflection; but I also wanted someone to talk to. It wasn't long before I looked forward to the Beast's daily visits, even before I had overcome my fear of him. It was difficult to completely forget fear of something as large as a bear, maned like a lion, and silent as the sun; but after a very few weeks of his company I found it was equally difficult not to like and trust him.

Even my makeshift bird feeder was successful. On the very first day I noticed that the seed had been disturbed, rearranged into little swirls and hollows that, I thought hopefully, were more likely to have been caused by birds' feet and beaks than by errant wind; although in this castle one was never sure. But the next morning I saw a tiny winged shadow leave the sill as I approached the window; and at the end of two weeks I had half a dozen regular visitors I recognized: three sparrows, a chaffinch, a little yellow warbler, and a diminutive black-and-white creature with a striped breast that I didn't recognize. They grew so tame that they would perch on my fingers and take grain from my hand, and chirp and whistle at me when I chirped and whistled at them. I never saw anything larger than a dove.

The weather over these enchanted lands was nearly always fine. Spring should have a good grasp on the world where my family still lived; there would be mud everywhere, and the trees would be putting out their first fragile green, and the shabby last year's grass would be displaced by this year's fresh growth. At the castle, the gardens remained perfect and undisturbed—by seasonal change, animal depredations, or anything else. Not only was there no sign of gardeners, visible or invisible, but there was never any sign of any need for gardeners; hedges never seemed to need trimming, nor flower beds weeding, nor trees pruning; nor did the little streams in their mosaic stone beds swell with spring floods.

The outlying lands where Greatheart and I rode were touched with the change of season; the snow patches disappeared from the ground, and new leaves appeared on the trees. But even here there was little mud; the ground thawed and grew softer under the horse's hoofs without turning marshy, and there was little dead vegetation from past seasons, either underfoot or on the bushes and trees. The fresh young green replaced nothing brown and weary, but grew on clean polished stems and branches.

Occasionally, however, it did rain. I woke up one morning a little over a fortnight after I first arrived, and noticed how dimly the sun shone through my window. I looked out and saw a gentle grey but persistent rain falling. The garden glimmered like jewels under water, or like a mermaids' city of which I was catching fantastic glimpses beneath the surface of a deep quiet lake. "Oh," I said sadly. This new vision of the castle and gardens was beautiful, but it meant postponing our morning walk. I dressed and ate slowly, then wandered listlessly downstairs, thinking to walk about a little indoors, and perhaps make a conciliatory visit to Greatheart, before settling down to a long morning of study.

The Beast was standing at the front doors, which were open. He stood with his back to me as I walked down the curved marble staircase; for a moment I thought he looked like Aeolus, standing at the mouth of his thundery cavern on the mountain of the gods; a warm wind sang around him, and came up to greet me on the stairs, smelling of a green land at the end of the world. As I reached the ground floor he turned around and said gravely, "Good morning, Beauty."

"Good morning, Beast," I answered, wondering a little, because I had only seen him in the evenings before. I walked down the hall and came to stand beside him in the doorway. "It's raining," I said, but he understood the question, because he answered:

"Yes, even here it rains sometimes." As if he thought

there was need for some explanation, he went on: "I've found that it doesn't do to tinker with the weather too much. The garden will take care of itself as long as I don't try to be too clever. Snow disappears in a night, you know, and it's never very cold here, but that's about all. Usually it rains after nightfall," he added apologetically.

"It does look very beautiful," I said. I knew by this time that his kindness was real, as was his interest in my welfare. It was very mean of me to boggle at rain, and it showed how selfish and spoiled I was becoming through having my least whim granted. "All misty and mysterious. I'm sorry I was sulky; of course it has to rain, even here."

"I thought, perhaps," he said hesitantly, "that you might like to see a bit more of the castle this morning, since you can't go out. I believe that there is quite a lot that you have missed."

I nodded and smiled wryly. "I *know* there is. I can't seem to keep the corridors straight in my head somehow, and as soon as I'm hopelessly lost, I turn a corner and there's my room again. So I never learn anything. I don't mean to complain," I added hastily. "It's just that I get lost so *very* quickly that I don't have the chance to see very much before they—er—send me home again."

"I quite understand," said the Beast. "The same used to happen to me."

Two hundred years, I thought, watching raindrops sliding slowly down the luminous pale marble.

"But I know my way around rather well by now, I think," he continued. There was a pause. The rain seeped into the raked sand of the courtyard till it sparkled like opal. "Is there anything in particular that you would like to see?"

"No," I said, and smiled up at him. "Anything you like."

With a guide, the great rooms that had blurred into surfeit before my dazzled eyes during my solitary rambles became clear again, full of individual wonders. After some time we came to a portrait gallery, the first I had seen in the castle; all the paintings I had looked at thus far had avoided depicting human beings in any detail. I paused to look at these more closely. The men and women were most of them handsome, and all of them very grand. I knew little about styles and techniques of painting, but it seemed to me that they were a series, extending over a considerable period of time, possibly several centuries. I thought I saw a family resemblance, particularly among the men: tall, strong, brown-haired and brown-eyed, and a bit grim about the mouth, and they all had a certain proud tilt of eyebrow and chin and shoulder. "This looks like a family," I said.

There were no recent portraits; the line seemed to have stopped a long time ago. "Who are they?" I said, studying the picture of a pretty woman, golden-haired and green-eyed, with a silly fluffy white lap dog, and trying to sound casual; it was the secret that hid behind the men's eyes I really wondered about.

The Beast was silent so long I looked at him inquiringly. It was more difficult to gaze at him steadily again after looking at all the handsome, proud painted human faces. "They are the family that have owned these lands for thousands of years, since time began, and before portraits were painted," he said at last.

He spoke in the same tone of voice that he had used in reply to all my other questions, yet for the first time in several days I was reminded of the undercurrent of thunder in his deep harsh voice, and remembered that he was a Beast. I shivered and dared ask no more.

I looked longest at the last painting in the long row: Beyond it the wall was decorated with scrolls and hangings, but there were no more portraits. This last one that held my attention was of a handsome young man, of my age perhaps; one hand held the bridle of a fine chestnut horse that was arching its neck and stamping. There was something rather terrible about this young man's beauty, though I could not say just where the dreadfulness lay. The hand on the bridle was clenched a little too tightly; the light in the eyes was a little too bright, as if the soul itself were burning. He seemed to watch me as I looked at him, watch me with all the intensity of those eyes; the other portraits I examined had flat painted eyes that behaved as they should, vaguely refusing to focus on their audience. For a moment I was frightened; then I raised my chin and stared back. This castle was a strange place, and probably not to be trusted, but I trusted the Beast; he would not let me be bewitched by any daub.

As I stared I began unwillingly to realize just how beautiful this young man was, with his curly brown hair, high forehead, and straight nose. His chin and neck were a perfect balance between grace and strength, he was broad-shouldered and evidently tall, and the hand holding the bridle was finely shaped. He was wearing velvet of the purest sapphire hue; the white lace at his throat and wrists made his skin golden. His beauty was extraordinary, even in this good-looking family; and the passion of his expression made him loom above me like a godling. I looked away at last, no longer afraid, but ashamed, remembering the undersized, sallow, snub-nosed creature he looked down upon.

"What do you think of him?" the Beast asked.

I glanced at the picture again briefly. I thought: The artist was a genius, to catch that fire-eaten look. He must have been exhausted when he was done; I'm tired after only a few minutes of looking at the finished work. "I think he died young," I said finally. A curious silence stepped in, took my words, and tapped and shook and rattled them together, as if they would ring clear as brass or silver; and then, disgusted, blew them away entirely.

I felt as if I were half-awakened from an uneasy sleep by the Beast's words: "Let me show you the library." We walked down a half flight of stairs; the Beast opened a door set in a pillared arch. I looked back for a moment, over his shoulder; the hall of paintings had faded to indecipherable, shadowy colors. But the young man of the last portrait lingered before my mind's eye in a way that disturbed me. I hesitated on the brink of trying to find out why; but my courage failed me, as it had when I had first faced his likeness. I told myself a little too firmly that I was reacting only to his extraordinary physical beauty, and fairly forced him out of my mind. I glanced up at the Beast and found him looking down at me, one hand still on the library door. Where do you fit into all this? I thought; what has happened to the handsome family that has owned this land since before portraits were painted? Are you a doorkeeper, a kind of silent Cerberus perhaps? And what marvels might you guard beyond those I see around me? And there my courage failed me a third time, because I suddenly remembered myself as a small and very ordinary mortal, far from home and family—alone except for this great Beast who stood beside me, within whose power I was caught, for ends I knew nothing of. I was afraid again, as I stared at the Beast, afraid much as I had been on the first night; but then it was as if my vision cleared. He was not the awful master here, but my friend and companion within the spellbound castle. He too had had to learn to find his way through the maze of rooms and corridors that now bewildered me; he had had to learn to cope with enchantments in unfamiliar languages. As he stared down at me I knew his eyes were kind, and a little anxious, even though I could not read the rest of his dark face. I smiled at him, the handsome family forgotten, then turned and went through the door.

This single room of the library was as large as our whole house in the city had been, and I could see more book-filled rooms through open doors in all directions, including a balcony overhead, all built from floor to high ceiling with bookshelves. "Oh *my,*" I said. "How do you reach the top shelves?"

A miniature staircase, complete with a banister on one side, rolled up to me; I had the feeling that it would have cleared its throat respectfully if it had had a throat to clear. "You remind me of our butler in the city," I said to it. "He stood at attention just the way you're doing now. Do you clean silver as well as he did?" It moved in a half circle backwards, and I thought it was probably eyeing me in confusion.

"Don't distress it," said the Beast mildly. "It will try to clean silver to please you, and it isn't built for it."

I laughed. "Pardon me, sir," I said to the waiting staircase. "I do *not* wish you to clean silver." It settled down on its wheels with the faintest sigh of condensing springs. "Do you ever get yourself in messes by wishing inappropriate things?" I said to the Beast.

"No," he replied. "My orders are obeyed, not my wishes."

I turned my head away unhappily, but the rows of books tugged unrepentantly at the edges of my sight. I walked like one bewitched to the nearest shelf. "I didn't know there were so many books in the *world*," I said caressingly, and the Beast's answer was heard only in my ear and did not register in my brain: "Well, in fact, there aren't," he said.

I pulled a volume down at random, and opened it to the title page. "*The Complete Poems of Robert Browning*," I read aloud, puzzled. "I've never even heard of him." Pride before a fall, I thought. So much for my scholarship. The Beast said nothing; when I looked up at him he was watching me with a curious, intent expression. I put Browning back, and picked out another book. This one was called *The Adventures of Sherlock Holmes*. The next one was *The Screwtape Letters*. Then *Kim*. "Rudyard Kipling," I said in despair. "This is a name? I've never heard of *any* of these people. And the paper is funny, and the shape of the letters. What's wrong?"

"Nothing is wrong," said the Beast; he sounded pleased, which I didn't like, assuming that he was amused at my discomfiture. "This library is—well—" He paused. "Most of these books haven't been written yet." I looked at him stupidly, *Kim* still in my hand. "But don't worry, they will be," he said. There was a pause. "You might try the Browning," he suggested gently. "It shouldn't be too confusing. I'm very fond of his poetry myself."

I should have long been past being shocked by anything in this castle, but I now discovered that I wasn't. My dazed brain grasped at something more easily sensible. "You—you do read then," I said, and added before I thought: "You can turn pages?"

The earthquaking rumble that served the Beast for a chuckle washed over me briefly, lifting the hair on the back of my neck. "Yes, after a fashion. You'll find that some of my favorite books are somewhat battered about the corners." I looked at him, slowly collecting my wits. "Look," he said. He held one arm out, shook the lace back from his wrist, stretched the fingers of the hand. Their tips glittered. "They're sort of semi-retractable; not nearly so well-designed as a cat's," he said. The fingers quivered and about six inches of shining curved claw suddenly appeared. The daggers that served as index finger and thumb curved and met. "The temptation is always to rip things up a bit when my clumsiness prevents me from turning a page neatly." The claws clicked lightly together. He sounded almost merry; he rarely spoke of himself, and then his tone was usually grim and sad.

I was not frightened, but I was ashamed. "I'm sorry," I said.

The claws retreated, and his arm dropped. "Don't

be," he said. "I don't mind telling you." He looked at me. "But perhaps you mind being told."

"No," I said automatically; and then my slow thoughts caught up with me and told me that this was true. "No, I don't mind." We looked at each other for a moment. The sun shone through a window, then made its delicate, fawn-footed way across the broad inlaid floor, and found the Beast's blue velvet shoulders to set on fire. "The sun," I said abruptly. "Look, it's stopped raining." I went over to the window; the Beast joined me. The garden gleamed; the towers of the ancient castle looked young again, baptized by young rain. "I can take Greatheart out after all."

"Yes," said the Beast. "I am sure he is looking for you." The light-heartedness was gone. "I will say farewell to you now," he continued. "I will see you this evening." He turned away.

"No—wait," I said, and put a hand out, but did not quite touch the velvet arm. He paused and looked back at me. "Wait," I repeated. "Greatheart likes whomever I like. Come with us."

The Beast shook his head. "Thank you for the kindness of your offer, but no. It is not necessary, and I assure you it would not work. I will see you this evening."

"Please," I said.

"Beauty," he said, "I can deny you nothing. Do not ask this. Greatheart loves you. Do not break his trust in you for no reason."

"Please," I said. "I am asking."

There was a pause, but at last he said, as if the words were dragged from him like a blessing from a black magician, "Very well. I am sorry for this."

"Come then," I said. I went out through the door we had come in, and turned down the hall, away from the paintings. The Beast followed. In the usual fashion, I found my room around the next corner, and from there I could easily find the way down the great staircase to the front doors. I paused there and waited for the Beast. When he did not speak his mere presence could be oppressive; I felt as if I were waiting for a stormcloud to catch me up.

We went out into the courtyard together. The air was cool and damp against my cheek. "Not in the stable," said the Beast. "Give the poor brute room. I will wait for you here." He walked away from the stable wing to a bench at the edge of the garden on the opposite side, just inside the courtyard, and sat down. I went to fetch my horse.

He was glad to see me, and eager to go outside. I found that now that I had committed myself to this venture, I was frightened, and unhappily inclined to believe the Beast's predictions. Greatheart had too much sense to walk into the dragon's mouth merely because I asked him to. But it was too late now. After a moment's reflection, I put on his saddle and bridle. I had no chance at all of arguing with him from the ground with nothing but a halter and rope for persuasion; mounted, at least I could stay with him—probably—until he could be reasoned with. Oh dear. Why did the Beast have to sound so forlorn just at the wrong moment?

Greatheart was a bit puzzled at being saddled at this hour, but he was willing enough. He was snorting with enthusiasm and pulling at the reins as the stable door opened for us.

I saw the change at once, and mounted hastily at the threshold. As soon as his head emerged, he flared his nostrils and blew, and swung his head towards the bench where the Beast sat. I could feel him turn to iron under my hand, and there was a glimpse of white around his eye. The door closed noiselessly behind us; the last little breath of warm hay-scented air stirred my hair. Greatheart hadn't taken his eyes off the Beast; he was blowing unhappily, and spume began to form on his lips. I tightened the girths. Well, here we go, I thought, and gathered up the reins.

It took us fifteen minutes to cross a courtyard two hundred feet wide. The horse's shoulders and flanks were soon dark with sweat; but he went in the direction I insisted on. I whispered to him as he walked, and for the first time in his life he did not cock an ear back at me to listen. He would obey me—but only just; his entire concentration rested on the dark figure sitting on a white marble bench, its arms stretched out across the seat's back.

Fifty feet from Nemesis Greatheart stopped and would go no farther; we stood like stone in a silent battle of wills. My knees were pressed into the horse's sides till my legs ached, and my hands on the reins urged him forwards; but his mouth was frozen on the bits, and I could feel a tiny quiver of panic, deep inside him. "Don't move," I said, panting, to the Beast. "This is harder than I was expecting."

"I won't," said the Beast. "I did not believe you would come so far."

At the sound of the Beast's voice, Greatheart's nerve broke. He reared up so wildly I threw myself forwards, fearing that he would go over backwards, and his neigh was a scream, sharp as shipwreck. Still on his hind legs, he whirled, nearly unseating me, and in two bounds he was back on the far side of the courtyard it had taken us so long to cross. I found myself yelling, "No, you great ox, stop it, listen to me, rot you, listen to me!" and when I untangled my hands from his mane and pulled again on the reins, his ears flickered and he stopped, shuddering and heaving as if he were at his strength's end after a long gallop. He turned as he stopped, to look back in terror at the enemy, threw up his head, and took several unhappy steps sideways. The Beast had stood up, presumably when Greatheart had bolted. Now that it seemed that I was more or less in control again, he slowly resumed his seat.

I let the reins fall on the horse's neck, and leaned forwards to run my hands through his silky mane and down his wet shoulders; and stiffly, as if he had almost forgotten how, he arched his neck and slowly bowed his head. I talked to him, telling him he was a great stupid creature and very silly, and that I knew best; be quiet, relax, have no fear, have no fear, have no fear. His ears flickered back and forth, and he swung a restless head towards the Beast; then at last he stood still, his ears back to listen to me, and I felt him slowly return from cold iron to warm flesh. "Okay," I said at last. "We'll try again."

And I gathered up the reins and turned him towards the Beast.

He walked slowly this time too, but only as if he were very, very tired, and his head hung low. He paused once again about fifty feet away from the edge of the courtyard and raised his head a few inches; but when I nudged him forwards he went without demur. "It's all right now," I said to the Beast. "He's ashamed of himself, and he'll do as I say."

The last step brought us to the bench; and with a gesture half of resignation and half of despair, Greatheart dropped his head till his muzzle touched the Beast's knee. "Merciful God," murmured the Beast. Greatheart's ears shot forwards at the sound of his voice, but he didn't move.

I dismounted, and Greatheart turned his head to press it against my breast, leaving streaks of grey foam on my shirt, and I rubbed behind his ears. "You see?" I said to either or both of them, as if I had been sure all along of the outcome. "That wasn't so bad."

"I was fond of horses, once," said the Beast; and his words had a distant sound, as if they echoed down a cold corridor of centuries. I looked at him inquiringly, but said nothing. He replied in answer to what I did not say: "Yes;

I have not always been as you see me now." Not Cerberus, then, I thought absently, still petting my horse; but I did not pursue the question any further. For my own limited peace of mind I preferred to admire the small victory I had just won, and leave the castle's immense secrets to themselves.

The Beast left us shortly after this; I was a little disappointed, but I made no move to stop him. I ate my lunch alone, and went out early to take Greatheart for his afternoon ride. We took it very easy that day, and when I put him away, the horse was anxious to be petted and soothed at great length. After he had been groomed hair for hair several times over, I sat between his forelegs and told him silly stories, as if to a child at bedtime, while he investigated my face and hair with his nose. At last he was calm and happy again, and I could leave him. The Beast was waiting for me outside, silhouetted against an amber-and-primrose-colored sky. "Greatheart and I have been having a long conversation," I explained, and the Beast nodded without comment.

That night as the whistling breeze unrolled my bedclothes to tuck snugly under my chin I heard the voices I'd heard before on that dreadful first night in the castle. Several times over the last weeks I had thought

I heard them, but always just at the edge of sleep, and usually only a few words: "Good night, child, and sweet dreams," and once, "For heaven's sake leave the child alone," whereupon the quilt had abruptly left off tucking in its corners.

"Well," I heard. "Are you satisfied yet? No, I shouldn't ask that. Do you begin to have hope? Are you comforted? You see how well it's going."

There was a melancholy sigh. "Oh, yes, already it's going better than I dared hope, and yet you know it's not enough. It's too much, really it is, too much to ask, how can such a little thing understand? How can she possibly guess? There's nothing to guide her; it's not allowed."

"You fidget yourself too much," said the practical voice, but with sympathy.

"I can't help it. You know it's impossible."

"It was made to be impossible," the first voice said grimly. "But you needn't give up on that account."

"Oh dear, oh dear, if only we could help, even a little," the melancholy voice went on.

"But we can't," said the first voice patiently. "In the first place, she can't hear us; and even if she could, we are bound to silence." Fuzzy with sleep, I thought: I know who she reminds me of—my first governess, Miss

Dixon, who taught me my alphabet, and to recognize countries on the globe before I could read the printed names; and who was the first of many to fail to teach me to sew a straight seam. Now this voice and its invisible owner brought her back to me with sudden clarity: dear, kind, and above all practical Miss Dixon, who disliked fairy tales and disapproved of witches, who believed that magicians invariably exaggerated their abilities; and once, exasperated at my favorite game of playing dragons, which involved much jumping out of trees, told me rather sharply that a creature as big and heavy as a dragon probably spent most of its life on the ground, wings or no wings. Hers was not a personality I would have expected to find in an enchanted castle.

"Yes, oh I know, I know. It's probably just as well, because if we could talk to her it would be just too tempting, and then even the last hope would be gone. . . . Good night, dear heart. It doesn't hurt to wish her good night," the voice added, a little defensively. "Maybe she can feel it, somehow."

"Maybe she can," said the first voice. "Good night then, child, and sleep well."

I found myself straining to say, But I can hear you, I can, please talk to me—what is it I can't understand?

What is impossible? What last hope? But I couldn't open my mouth, and with the effort I suddenly woke up, to find a moon half full staring in through the tall window at me; the fringe of the bed-curtains made a filigree pattern of the light that fell on my bed. I stared back at the serene white half circle and its attendant constellations for a little while, and then fell into a dreamless sleep.

3

Spring grew slowly into summer. I no longer needed a cloak on the long afternoon rides, and the daisies in the meadows grew up to Greatheart's knees. I finished rereading the *Iliad* and started the *Odyssey*; I still loved Homer, but Cicero, whom I read in a spirit of penance, I liked no better than I had several years ago. I read the *Bacchae* and *Medea* over and over again so many times that I knew them by heart. I also found my way back to the great library at the end of the hall of paintings, and read the Browning that the Beast had recommended. On the whole I liked the poems, even if they were a little obscure in places. Emboldened, I tried *The Adventures of Sherlock*

Holmes, but I had to give that up in a few pages, because I could make nothing of it. Then quite by accident, or at least it seemed so, I discovered a long shelf of wonderful stories and verses by a Sir Walter Scott; and I read a book called *The Once and Future King* twice, although I still liked Malory better. I stayed away from the hall of paintings. The castle, as usual, ordered itself to the convenience of my comings and goings, and the library was now regularly to be found down one short corridor and up a flight of stairs from my room.

After that day when I introduced the Beast and Greatheart to each other, the Beast occasionally joined us on our morning walks. At first Greatheart was uneasy, although he gave me no more trouble; but after a few weeks Greatheart was nearly as comfortable as I was in the Beast's company. I let the big horse wander free, without halter or rope, as I had done at home; and I noticed that he kept me between himself and the Beast, and the Beast never offered to touch him.

Sometimes too the Beast would find me in the library, where I was sitting on my feet in a huge wing chair reading *The Bride of Lammermoor* or *The Ring and the Book*. Once he found me smiling foolishly over "How They Brought the Good News from Ghent to Aix," and asked me to read it aloud. I hesitated. I was sitting by the window, where my favorite chair had obligingly arranged itself, my elbow on the ivy-edged stone sill. The Beast turned away from me long enough to call a chair up to him, which was joined a moment later by a footstool with four ivory legs, bowed like the forelegs of a bulldog. He sat down and looked at me expectantly. There didn't seem to be any opportunity for nervousness on my part, so I put my hesitations aside and read it. "Now it's your turn," I said, and passed the book to him.

He held it as if it were a butterfly for a moment, then leaned back and began to turn the pages—with dexterity, I noticed—and then made me laugh with his sly reading of "Soliloquy of the Spanish Cloister." I didn't realize it at the time, but that was the beginning of a tradition; most days after that we took turns reading to each other. Once after several weeks of a daily chapter of *Bleak House,* he did not come one day, and I missed him sadly. I scolded him for his neglect when I saw him at sunset that evening. He looked pleased and said, "Very well. I shan't miss again."

This brief exchange made me think, whether I would or no. I wondered that we didn't tire of each other's company; perhaps even more I wondered that I *sought* his.

We saw each other several hours of every day; yet I at least always looked forwards to the next meeting, and his visits never seemed long. Part of it, I supposed, was that we were each other's only alternative to solitude; but I could admit that this wasn't all. I tried not to wonder too much, and to be grateful. This idyll was not at all what I had imagined during that last month at home with a red rose keeping secret silent watch over the parlour.

There were only two flaws in my enjoyment of this new life. The worst was my longing for home, for the sight of my family; and I found that the only way I could control this sorrow was not to think of them at all, which was almost as painful as the loss itself. The other was that every evening after supper, when I stood up from the long table in the dining hall and prepared to go upstairs to my room, the Beast asked: "Beauty, will you marry me?" Every evening, I answered, "No," and left the room at once. The first few weeks I looked over my shoulder as I hastened upstairs, fearing that he would be angry, and would follow me to put his question more forcefully. But he never did. The weeks passed, and with them my fear, which was replaced by friendship and even a timid affection. I came to dread that nightly question for quite a different reason. I did not like to refuse him the only thing he ever asked of me. My "No" grew no less certain, but I said it quietly and walked upstairs feeling as if I had just done something shameful. We had such good times together, and yet they always came to this, at every day's final parting. I knew I was fond of him, but the thought of marrying him remained horrible.

After the Beast had told me, at the beginning of my stay, that I should not allow myself to be bullied by the invisible servants, and specifically by the bowls and platters that served me at dinner, I began to enjoy occasionally expressing a preference. That wonderful table would never have offered me the same dish twice; but while I reveled in the variety, I also sometimes demanded a repetition. There was a dark treacly spice cake that I liked very much, and asked for several times. Sometimes it burst into being like a small exploding star, several feet above my head, and settled magnificently to my plate; sometimes a small silver tray with a leg at each of five or six corners would leap up and hurry towards me from a point far down the table.

One evening near mid-summer I asked for my favorite cake again. The Beast sat, as usual, to my right as I headed the immense table. There was a wine-glass in front of him, and a bottle of white wine the color of moonlight we were sharing. After many weeks of my asking him if there wasn't something he would eat or drink with me, he had admitted that he enjoyed a glass of wine now and then. Most nights after that he had at least a few sips of whatever I was drinking, although I noticed that he never touched his glass when I was looking at him.

"You should try this," I said, cutting the cake with a silver knife.

"Thank you," said the Beast, "but as I have told you, I cannot wield knife and fork."

"You don't need to," I said. "Here, stop that," I said to the cake. I had cut a piece from the tray but when I laid the knife down it promptly sprang up again and was lifting the piece onto my plate. "I'll do that." I picked up the slice of cake and bit into it. "Like this," I said to the Beast around a mouthful.

"Don't tease me," said the Beast. "I cannot. Besides, my—er—mouth isn't set up for chewing."

"Neither is Honey's," I said. I had told him about Melinda's ugly mastiff. "And she will *inhale* cakes and pies and cookies by the hundredweight if they are left unguarded. This is really very good. Open your mouth." I stood up, cake in hand, and walked around the corner of the table. The Beast looked at me warily. I felt like the mouse confronted by the lion in the fable, and grinned. "Come; it won't hurt."

"I—" began the Beast, and I pushed the morsel of cake between his teeth. I turned away and went back to my chair and busied myself cutting another piece without looking at him, remembering that he would not drink if I watched. After a moment I thought I heard him swallow. I gave him another minute, and looked up. There was the most extraordinary expression in his eyes. "Well?" I said briskly.

"Yes, it is good," said the Beast.

"Then have a little more," I said, and whisked around the table to stand by his chair again before he could say anything. He hesitated a moment, his eyes searching my face; then he opened his mouth obediently. After a minute he said dolefully, "It will probably disagree with me."

"It will do nothing—" I began indignantly, and realized he was laughing silently at me. We both laughed aloud, till the table danced in sympathy, and as I put my head back I saw the chandelier turning on its chain, winking and tinkling its crystal pendants.

"Oh my," I sighed at last. The teapot approached and poured me a cupful; tonight it was sweetened with orange peel, spiced with ginger. I drank in silence, enjoying the friendly warmth of tea and laughter. I set my cup down empty, and said: "It is time I went upstairs. What with one thing and another—Browning and Kipling, you know—I'm getting nowhere with Catullus."

"Beauty, will you marry me?" said the Beast.

The world was as still as autumn after winter's first snowfall, and as cold as three o'clock in the morning beside a deathbed. I pressed myself back in my chair and closed my eyes, my fingers clenching on the carved arms till the smooth scrolled edges pinched my skin. "No, Beast," I said, without opening my eyes. "Please—I am—very fond of you. I wish you wouldn't ask me this, for I cannot, cannot, marry you, and I don't like telling you no, and no, and no, again and again." I looked at him.

"I cannot help asking," he said, and there was an undertone to his voice that frightened and saddened me. He made a brusque gesture, and the wine-bottle toppled under his arm. He turned and caught it in mid-air with a grace that seemed inhuman to my troubled senses. He paused, looking at the bottle as if it were the future, his head and back bent.

"You—you are very strong, aren't you," I whispered.

"Strong?" he said in a queer, detached voice that did not sound like his own. "Yes, I am strong." He lingered on the last word as if he detested it. He straightened up in his chair and held the bottle at arm's length. His hand tightened on the bottle, and it snapped and shattered, the shards cascading to the table and splintering against silver and gold, and falling to the floor.

"Oh, you have hurt yourself!" I cried, jumping up. His hand was still closed, and mixed with the pale wine stain spreading across the tablecloth like the battle-ranks of an advancing army, darker drops were welling up from the tender web of flesh between thumb and index finger and running down his wrist, and spotting the white lace; and dripping to the table between the dark clenched fingers.

He stood up, and I checked my vague impulse to go to him, and stood shivering by my chair. He opened his hand, and a few more bits of glass fell to the table. He turned the hand palm up and looked at it. "It is nothing," he said. "Only that I am a fool." He strode off down the long table without looking at me; a door opened in a gloomy corner, and he was gone.

After a moment I left the dining hall and went upstairs. My long stiff embroidered skirts seemed heavier than usual, the sleeves and shoulders more binding. There was no sign of the Beast.

My evening was ruined. I liked reading by an open fire,

so my room arranged to be cool enough that a fire on the hearth was pleasant to sit beside. But tonight I couldn't concentrate on Catullus, who seemed dull and petulant; I couldn't find a comfortable position in my chair; even the fire seemed sullen and brooding. The first flaw in my happiness here, always the stronger of the two, struck me with particular force. I thought of my family. Richard and Mercy were over a year old by now; they were probably walking, and might have said their first words. They would have no recollection of the aunt who had left over four months ago. I could see Hope, smiling, playing with the babies, tickling their faces and bare feet with daisies. I thought of Ger, black to the elbows, with smudges on his face, holding a horse's hoof balanced between his knees in his leather apron. I thought of Grace in the kitchen, her face delicately flushed with the heat, and a golden curl or two escaping from its net. Then I saw my father, whistling between his teeth, whittling a long pole so that the chips flew. My eyes filled with tears; but they didn't spill over till I suddenly saw the house covered with roses, huge, beautiful roses of many colors; somehow that was the worst of all. I laid my face in my arms and sobbed.

I woke up the next morning still tired; a headache pricked behind my eyes, and the fresh sunlight pouring through my window like a golden gift looked flat and sour. The mood refused to lift. I ate, and walked in the gardens, and read, and talked to the Beast, and galloped Greatheart through the green meadows; but the picture of a small dun-colored house, covered with hundreds of climbing roses, drummed in my head and let me see nothing else.

At supper I was silent, as I had been for most of the day. The Beast had asked me several times if I was unwell, if there was something troubling me; I had put him off each time with a few brusque or impertinent words. Each time he looked away and forbore to press me. I felt guilty for the way I treated him; but how could I tell him what was hurting me? I had agreed to come and live in his castle to save my father's life, and I must abide by my promise. The Beast's subsequent kindness to me led me to hope that one day he might set me free; but I did not think I could rightfully ask. At least not yet, after only four months. But I longed so much to see my family that I could only remember to hold to my promise; I could not always do it cheerfully.

I was staring into my teacup when the Beast asked me once more: "Beauty. Please. Tell me what is wrong. Perhaps I can help."

I looked up, irritated, my mouth open to tell him to leave me alone—please: But something in his expression stopped me. I flushed, ashamed of myself, and looked down again.

"Beauty," repeated the Beast.

"I—I miss my family," I muttered.

The Beast leaned back in his chair and there was a pause. "You would leave me then?" he said; and the hopelessness in his voice shook me even from the depths of my self-pity. I remembered for the first time since my home-sickness had seized me the night before that he had no family to wish for. "It is rather lonesome here sometimes," he had said at our first meeting; and I had been able to pity him then, before I had learned to like him. My friendship was worth little if I could forget it, and him, so quickly.

"I would be very sorry never to see you anymore," I said. "But you have been so kind to me that I have—I have occasionally wondered perhaps if—perhaps if after some term is completed, that you would—might let me go. I would still wish to remain your friend." He was silent, and I went falteringly on: "I know it is too soon yet—I have only been here a few months. I know I shouldn't have mentioned it. It is very ungrateful of me—and dishonourable," I said miserably. "I didn't want to say anything—I wasn't going to—but you kept asking what was wrong—and I miss them so very much," and I caught myself up on a sob.

"I cannot let you go," said the Beast. I looked at him. "Beauty, I'm sorry." He seemed about to say something more, but I gave him no time.

"Cannot?" I breathed. There was something interminable in that short word. I stood up and backed a few steps away from the table. The Beast sat, with his right hand on the table, the white bandage on it almost covered by the waves of lace. He looked at me; I could not see his eyes; the world was turning a shimmering, dancing grey, like the inside of a snowflake. I blinked, and a voice I did not recognize as my own said: "Never let me go? Not ever? I will spend my entire life here—and never see anyone again?" And I thought: My life? He has been here two centuries. What is my life span likely to be here? The castle was a prison: The door would not open. "Dear God," I cried, "the door won't open. Let me out, let me out!" I raised my fists to pound on silent wooden panels that I seemed to see loom up in front of me, and then I knew no more.

I returned to consciousness slowly and piecemeal.

For the first few minutes I had no idea where I was; at first I supposed that I was at home, in bed. But that could not be; the pillow under my cheek was soft and slightly furry—velvet, I thought drowsily. Velvet. We have no velvet at home—except what the Beast sent in Father's saddlebags. The Beast. Of course. I was in the castle. I had been here for several months. Then I remembered, still dimly, that very recently I had been terribly unhappy; but I did not remember why. How could I be unhappy here? I thought. I have everything I want, and the Beast is very kind to me. A stray thought, less substantial than a wisp of smoke, suggested, The Beast loves me; but it dissolved immediately and I forgot about it. Just now I was very comfortable, and I did not want to move. I rubbed my cheek a little against the warm velvet. There was a curious odour to it; it reminded me of forests, of pine sap and moss and springwater, only with a wilder tang beneath it.

My memory began to return. I had been unhappy because I was home-sick. The Beast had said that he could not let me go home. Then I must have fainted. It occurred to me that the velvet my face rested on was heaving and subsiding gently, like someone breathing; and my fingers were wrapped around something that felt very much like the front of a coat. There was a weight across my shoulders that might have been an arm. I was leaning against the whatever-it-was, half sitting up. I turned my head a few inches, and caught a glimpse of lace, and beneath it a white bandage on a dark hand; and the rest of my mind and memory returned with a shock like a snowstorm through a window blown suddenly open.

I gasped, half a shriek, let go the velvet folds I was clutching, and pushed myself violently away. I found myself kneeling at the opposite end of a small cushioned sofa. This was the first time I saw him clumsy. He stood up and took a few stumbling steps backwards; he held out his hands and looked at me as though I hated him. "You fainted," he said; his voice was a rough whisper. "I caught you before you reached the floor. You—you might have hurt yourself. I only wanted to lay you down somewhere that you could be comfortable." I stared at him, still kneeling, with my fingernails biting into the sofa cushions. I couldn't look away from him, but I did not recognize what I saw. "You—you clung to me," he said, and there was a vast depth of pleading in his voice.

I wouldn't listen. Something inside me snapped; I put my hands over my ears, half-fell off the couch, and ran; he moved out of my way as if I were a cannon-ball or a madwoman. A door opened in front of me and I bolted through it. I had to pause to look around me; this was the great front hall. He had carried me from the dining room to the huge drawing room opposite it. I picked up my skirts and ran upstairs to my room as if Charon himself had left his river to fetch me away.

I passed another bad night, pulling my bed to pieces, unable to sleep. When I did doze, I dreamed uneasily, and several times I saw the arrogant, handsome young man of the last portrait in the gallery by the library. He seemed to look through me, and mock me; except for the last time he appeared, when he was very much older, with grey in his hair, and lines of wisdom and sympathy drawn on his handsome face; and he looked at me sorrowfully, but said no word. I rose shortly before dawn, when the black rectangle of my window began to turn grey, and I could see the leading around the individual panes. I wrapped myself in a quilted dressing gown, a bright blue and crimson that did nothing for my bleak brown mood, and sat on the window seat to watch the sun rise. The pillows and blankets rearranged themselves in a subdued fashion, and only when I wasn't looking at them. I felt deserted—the breeze that attended me had left after putting me to bed the night before, and did not return to keep me company during my early vigil. Often before when I had had restless nights, it would fuss around me with cups of warm milk sweetened with honey, and lap robes, if I still insisted on getting up.

But my head was clear, strangely clear, for two nights of sleeplessness and emotional upheaval; in fact I felt more clear-headed than I could ever recall feeling before. Light-headed is more likely, I told myself severely. It's an ill wind, though: I seem to have been cured of the worst of my home-sickness, for the moment anyway. That will probably turn out to be an illusion though, too. I'm just numb with exhaustion. Exhaustion? Shock. Shock? Well, why? What is so inherently awful about being carried to a sofa?

I had avoided touching him, or letting him touch me. At first I had eluded him from fear; but when fear departed, elusiveness remained, and developed into habit. Habit bulwarked by something else; I could not say what. The obvious answer, because he was a Beast, didn't seem to be the right one. I considered this I did not get very far; but I thought I knew what Persephone must have felt after she ate those pomegranate seeds; and was then surprised by a sudden rush of sympathy for the dour King of Hell.

That curious feeling of clear-headedness increased with the light. Grey gave way to pink, and then to deep flushed rose edged with gold; there wasn't a cloud in the sky, and I could see the morning star shining like hope from the bottom of Pandora's box. I opened a section of the window and a little wind slipped inside to play with my rumpled hair and tickle me back into the beginnings of a good mood.

Then I heard the voices. There was a rustling about them, like too many stiff satin petticoats, and I looked around in surprise, half-expecting to see someone. "Oh dear, oh dear," said the melancholy voice. "Just look at that bed. I'm sure she hasn't had a wink of sleep all night. Here now"—more sharply—"what are you about? Pull yourselves together immediately!" The bedclothes started scrambling over one another, and the bedcurtains quivered anxiously.

"Don't be too hard on them," said the practical voice mildly. "They've had a rough night too."

"We *all* have," said the first voice. "Oh yes indeed. And look at her sitting beside that open window, with her robe all open at the neck, and nothing but a bit of lace for a nightgown! She'll catch her death!" I guiltily put a hand to my collar. "And her hair! Good heavens.

Has she been standing on her head?"

The voices—these were the voices I had heard several times, just before I had drifted into sleep or just after; I had never decided which. They were my invisible maidservants, my friendly breeze, the voices of plain common sense in this magic-ridden castle. They whisked around now, finding hot water in a fold in the air, putting it in a basin, laying towels beside it. Breakfast was laid out—"It is early, but she will certainly feel better after she has eaten"—and all the while they talked, discussing me: "How pale and pinched she looks! Tonight we must be sure she rests properly"; and the coming day, and my wardrobe, and the difficulties of getting the food decently cooked and the floors decently waxed, and so on.

I sat amazed, listening. At first I thought that I must be asleep and dreaming, in spite of the cold clean touch of the dawn; that would also explain the odd sense of preternatural clear-headedness—I might dream anything.

But the sun rose, and I washed my face and hands and ate breakfast, while the voices went on and I listened. The clink of plate and fork and teacup, and the taste of the food, decided me. I was awake; something else had happened to me in this castle where anything might happen. I wondered what else I might find that I could hear or see that had been hidden from me until now.

I almost said aloud: "I can hear you"—but I stopped myself. Perhaps if I pretended continued deafness I would learn what they had meant, when I had caught bits of their conversation—for I was now sure I had heard them—in the weeks past: "You know it's impossible." "It was made to be impossible." After breakfast, when they brought me a walking dress—did I catch the shimmer of something almost visible out of the corners of my eyes, as they blew around me?—I did say, aloud, "I missed you last night."

"Oh dear, she missed us, I knew she would, we've always been here before. But we couldn't leave him; I haven't seen him in such a temper since—oh, years and years. I'm always afraid he may do himself a mischief when he's in that state—not that *she* has anything to fear—but we've always stood by him in such moods, it seems safer, we don't really *help* anything but our presence is a *distraction*, I think, and anything is better than nothing at all."

"It is very difficult for him. Much more so than for us."

"Well, of course"—indignantly. "We're almost— volunteers; and invisibility isn't really so bad once you're accustomed to not seeing yourself *around,* you know. . . ."

"Yes, I know," the other voice said drily.

"It is certainly a good thing that that magician took himself off directly after he'd finished his nasty business here, or he *would* have been murdered. Nights like this past remind me of it. Although I never have understood why killing a magician like that—fiend—yes, *fiend*—should be counted as murder; after all, he's not even *human.*"

"Now, Lydia. That sort of talk will get you nowhere— and he would be angry if he heard you. If he knows better, surely we should."

"Oh, Bessie, I know, it's very wrong of me, but I sometimes—I just can't *help* it." The voice sounded near tears. "This can't *possibly* work."

"You may think what you like of course," the other voice said briskly, "but I shan't give up. And neither will he."

"No," said the melancholy voice, but in a tone so woebegone as to suggest that determination was only another aspect of the problem.

A faint jingly noise like a laugh. "She's a good girl, and bright enough. She'll figure it out in the end."

"The end is a very long time off," Lydia said gloomily.

"All the more reason to be hopeful; there's plenty of

time. And she's stronger than she knows—even if she understands nothing of it. You've seen the birds? They come to the garden now—and you know that that was expressly forbidden. Nothing—not even butterflies, not even birds. But we have birds now."

"That's true," Lydia said wistfully.

"Well then," said Bessie, as if the argument was won. "Now then, come along; there's a lot to be done before lunch." Invisible fingers patted my hair and shoulders, and the breeze whirled up and was gone.

All this made no sense to me at all. A magician? Well, if ever there was a place that was obviously under a spell, this was it. And the Beast—he must be the "he" they talked so much about. He must be under a spell too. He had said once, "I have not always been as you see me now." And they said that I was "bright enough": Were there clues, then, that I was supposed to be picking up, arranging into a pattern? Oh dear. I didn't know anything about magic, and spells, and things; such branches of learning were considered a little less than respectable by everyone I knew—nor very intellectually rewarding, so I had felt little interest in them. Surely that wasn't the method I was supposed to be looking for. But what else was there? I felt very stupid, notwithstanding Bessie's—

stubborn, it seemed to me—faith that everything would work out in the end.

I tackled something more readily accessible: "He" had been in a temper last night.

Sudden dismay clutched my stomach, and my breakfast somersaulted. Was he very angry with me then? . . . Not that *she* has anything to fear . . ." Lydia had said. Dismay and my breakfast subsided, but I was still worried; I didn't like the idea of his being angry with me—perhaps I *had* treated him badly last night. Perhaps I should apologize. What if he was so angry that I didn't see him today? I felt lonely at once, and ashamed of myself.

I took the peacock-tin that held birdseed to the window. I leaned outside and whistled, scattering some seed on the sill as I did so. Butterflies and birds were forbidden; I was stronger than I knew, although I didn't know why. I sighed. I certainly didn't know why.

Little dark shadows crossed my face, and then I felt tiny feet on my head, and a sparrow perched on my outstretched hand. "Here, come down from there," I said, gently dislodging the chaffinch sitting on my head. We discussed the weather and the possibility of rain in chirps and blinks, and I tried to lure a robin to take seed from my hand, but he only cocked his head and looked at me.

No birds were allowed. Maybe these weren't real birds at all, but figments invented by the castle, or by the Beast, because I'd wanted birds. They looked real; the prick of their tiny claws was real. There were never very many of them—whatever that meant. And it was true, too, that recently I had heard birdsongs sometimes when I was out riding Greatheart. Maybe the spell was weakening? Maybe I wouldn't have to do anything heroic after all.

I had been sitting with the birds perhaps ten minutes when I began to feel uneasy. Uneasy was perhaps too strong a word. It was like trying to catch the echo of a sound so faint I wasn't sure it existed. Something existed that was niggling at the edge of my consciousness. I turned my head this way and that, seeking some plainer hint. No; it wasn't so much like a sound as like a teasing whiff of something, something that reminded me of forests, of pine sap and springwater, but with a wilder tang beneath it. The birds were still pecking unconcernedly around my fingers, along the sill.

"Beast," I called. "You're here—somewhere. I can feel it. Or something." I shook my head. There was a brief vision, behind my eyes, of him gathering himself together to materialize out of my sight, around a corner of the castle, before he walked around it in normal fashion and came to stand beneath my window. The birds flew away as soon as he had appeared—before he walked around the corner, and I could see him. "Good morning, Beauty," he said.

"Something's happened to me," I said like a child seeking reassurance. "I don't know what it is. I've felt peculiar all morning. How did I know you were near?"

He was silent.

"You know something of it," I said still listening to my new sixth sense.

"I can see that your new clarity of perception will create difficulties for me," he said lightly.

My room was on the second storey, over a very tall first storey, so I was looking down more than twenty feet to the top of his head. He had not looked up at me since he had wished me good morning. The grey in his hair seemed to reproach me for not being cleverer in understanding the spell that was laid on him, in not being of any use to him. Today he was wearing dark-red velvet, the color of sunset and roses, and cream-colored lace.

"Beast," I said gently. "I—want to apologize for my behaviour last night. It was very rude of me. I know you were only trying to help."

He looked up then, but I was too far away, even

leaning down over the sill with my elbows on the edge and my hands dangling, to read any expression on that dark face. He looked down again, and there was a pause. "Thank you," he said at last. "It's not necessary, but—well—thank you."

I sat farther out on the window ledge, spraying him with birdseed as he stood below. "Oh—er, sorry," I said. His face split into a white smile, and he said, "Aren't you coming for your walk in the garden? The sun is getting high," and he brushed cracked corn and sunflower seeds from his shoulders.

"Of course," I said, and slid back into my room, and was downstairs and outside in the courtyard, running towards the stable, in a moment. I let Greatheart out, and he roamed on ahead of us like an oversized dog, while the Beast and I walked behind. When the horse had found a meadow to his taste and was settled down to some serious grazing, I sat down on a low porphyry wall and looked at the Beast, who avoided my gaze.

"You know something about what's happened to me," I said, "and I want to know what it is."

"I don't know exactly," said the Beast, looking at Greatheart. "I have some idea of it."

I curled my feet up beside me on the wall. The Beast

was still standing, hands in pockets, half turned away from me. "Well?" I said. "What's your idea?"

"I'm afraid you won't like it, you see," said the Beast apologetically. He sat down at last, but kept his eyes on the horse.

"Well?" I said again.

The Beast sighed. "How shall I explain? You look at this world—my world, here, as you looked at your old world, your family's world. This is to be expected; it was the only world, and the only way of seeing, that you knew. Well; it's different here. Some things go by different rules. Some of them are easy—for example, there is always fruit on the trees in the garden, the flowers never fade, you are waited on by invisible servants." With a little tremor of laughter in his voice he added: "And many of the books in the library don't exist. But there are many things here that your old habits and skills have left you unprepared for." He paused. "I wondered, before you came, how you'd react—if you came. Well, I can't blame you; you were tricked into coming here. You have no reason to trust me."

I started to say something, in spite of not wanting to interrupt him for fear that he would not continue; but he shook his head at me and said, "Wait. No, I know, you've gotten used to the way I look, as much as anyone can, and my company amuses you, and you're grateful that your imprisonment here isn't as direful as you were anticipating—being served for dinner with an apple in your mouth, or a windowless dungeon far underground, or whatever." I blushed and looked down at my hands. "I've never liked *Faerie Queen*," he added irrelevantly. "It gives so many things a bad name.

"But I don't blame you," he continued. "As I said, you have no reason to trust me, and excellent reason not to. And in not trusting me, you trust nothing here that you cannot perceive on your old terms. You refuse to acknowledge the existence of anything that is too unusual. You don't see it, you don't hear it—for you it doesn't exist." He frowned thoughtfully. "From what you've told me, a little strangeness leaked through to you, your first night here, when you looked out your window. It frightened you—I quite understand this; it used to frighten me too—and you've avoided seeing anything else since."

"I—I haven't meant to," I said, distressed at this picture of myself.

"Not consciously, perhaps; but you have resisted me with all your strength—as any sane person would, when confronted with a creature like me." He paused again. "You know, the first drop of hope I tasted was that day I first showed you the library—when you were confronted with the works of Browning, and of Kipling, and you saw them. You might not have; you might have seen only Aeschylus and Caesar and Spenser, and authors you could have known in your old world." He went on as if talking to himself: "Later I realized that this was only a reflection of your love and trust for books; it had nothing to do with me, or with my castle and its other wonders. And the birds came to you; that seemed a hopeful sign. But they came because of the strength of your longing for your old home. But perhaps it was a beginning nonetheless."

He was silent for so long that I thought he would say no more, and I began to consider what sort of question to put to him next. But there was a strange quality to my sight that distracted me—a new depth or roundness, which seemed to vary depending on what I was looking at. Greatheart looked as he always had, large and dapplegrey and patient and lovable. But the grass he waded through caught the sunlight strangely, and seemed to move softly in response to something other than wind. When I looked up, the forest's black edge shivered and ran like ink on wet paper. It reminded me of the spidery quaking shadows I had seen from my window on my first night in the castle; but there was no dread to what I was, or wasn't, seeing now. This is silly, I thought; I don't suppose you really *see* the sort of thing he's talking about. What's wrong with my eyes? I found myself blinking and frowning if I looked steadily at the Beast, too; it wasn't that he looked any less huge or less dark or less hairy, but there was some difference. And how do I know whether I should see the sort of thing he's talking about or not? There was something wrong, that first night. There's something wrong now.

"Last night," he began again at last, "when you fainted, you were helpless, for good or ill. I carried you to a couch in the next room, I was going to call your servants, and leave you alone. But when I tried to set you down, you murmured in your sleep, and held on to my coat with both hands." He stood up, took a few paces away from me, a few paces back. "For a few minutes you were content—even happy—that I held you in my arms. Then you remembered, and ran away in panic. But it's those few minutes of sympathy, I think, that caused whatever change you're noticing now."

"Am I always going to know when you're nearby now?" I said, a little wistfully.

"I don't know. I should think it likely. I always know where you are, near or far. Is that all it is—that you were aware of me when you couldn't see me?"

I shook my head. "No. My vision is funny. My color sense is confused somehow. And you look funny."

"Mmm," he said. "I shouldn't worry about it if I were you. As I told you at our first meeting, you have nothing to fear. Would you like to go back now?"

I nodded assent and we turned and walked slowly back towards the castle. Greatheart tore up a few last hasty mouthfuls and followed. I had a great deal to ponder, and did not speak; nor did the Beast say anything.

The rest of the day passed as my days usually did. I did not again mention my new strange sense of things, and by the end of the afternoon the new crystalline quality to the air, the way the flower petals shaded off into some color I couldn't quite put a name to, and the way I was hearing things that weren't strictly sounds had, by and large, ceased to disturb me. That evening's sunset was the most magnificent that I had ever seen; I was stunned and enthralled by its heedless beauty and remained staring at the sky till the last shreds of dim pink had blown away, and the first stars were lit and hung in their appointed places. I turned away at last. "I'm sorry," I said to the

Beast, who stood a little behind me. "I've never seen such a sunset. It—it took my breath away."

"I understand," he replied.

I went upstairs to dress for dinner, still bemused by what I had just observed, and found an airy, gauzy bit of lace and silver ribbons draped across the bed and gleaming in its own pale light. A corner of the skirt lifted briefly as I entered, as though a hand had begun to raise it and then changed its mind.

"Oh for heaven's sake," I said in disgust, recalled from my visionary musings with a bump. "We've been through all this dozens of times before. I won't wear anything like this. Take it away." The dress was lifted by the shoulders till it hung like a small star in my chamber, and for all my certainty that I would not wear it, I did look at it a little longingly. It was very beautiful; more so, it seemed to me, than any of the other wonderful clothes my high-fashion-minded breeze had tried to put on me.

"Well?" I said sharply. "What are you waiting for?"

"This is going to be difficult," said Lydia's voice. If I hadn't been accustomed, until that day, to not hearing them, their present silence would have seemed ominous to me. Even the satin petticoats were subdued. I was suddenly uneasy, wondering what they had planned for me. The dress was wafted over to lie negligently across an open wardrobe door, and I was assisted out of my riding clothes. I was still shaking my hair loose from its net when there was a moment of confusion, like being caught in a cloud or a cobweb, and I emerged from it pushing my wild hair off my face and found that they had disobediently wrapped me in the shimmering bit of nothing I had ordered back into the closet. .

"What are you *doing*?" I said, surprised and angry. "I won't wear this. Take it off." My hands searched for laces to untie, or buttons, but I could find nothing; it fitted me as if it had been sewn on—perhaps it had. "No, no," I said. "What is this? I said *no.*" Shoes appeared on my feet; the golden heels were set with diamond chips, and bracelets of opals and pearls began to grow up my arms. "*Stop* it," I said, really angry now. My hair twisted up, and I reached up and pulled a diamond pin out of it till it tumbled down around my shoulders and back; the pin I threw on the floor. My hair cascading down around me startled me as I realized that it was brushing bare skin. "Good heavens," I said, shocked, looking down; there was hardly enough bodice to deserve the name. Sapphires and rubies appeared on my fingers. I pulled them off and sent them to join the diamond hair-pin. "You shan't get away with this," I said between my teeth, and kicked off the shoes. I hesitated to rip the dress off; I didn't like to damage it, angry as I was, and again I tried to find a way out of it. "This is a dress for a princess," I said to the listening air. "Why must you be so silly?"

"Well, you *are* a princess," said Lydia, and she sounded as if she were panting a little. Bessie said: "I suppose we must start somewhere, but this is very discouraging." "Why is she so stubborn?" asked Lydia, plaintively. "It's a beautiful dress."

"I don't know," replied Bessie, and I felt a quick surge of their determination, and this angered me even more.

"It is a beautiful dress," I said wildly, as my hair wound up again and the pin flew back to its place, and the shoes, and the rings to theirs; "And that's why I won't wear it; if you put a peacock's tail on a sparrow, he's still a brown little, wretched little, drab little *sparrow,*" and as a net of moonbeams settled around my shoulders and a glittering pendant curled lovingly around my neck, I sat down in the middle of the floor and burst into tears. "All right, I don't seem to be able to stop you," I said between sobs, "but I will *not* leave the room." I wept myself to silence and then sat, still on the floor, with my abundant skirts anyway around and under me, staring into the fire. I took the pendant off, not in any hope that it would stay off, but just to see what it was: It was a golden griffin, wings spread and big ruby eyes shining, about twice the size of the ring I wore every day and kept beside my bed at night. For some reason it made my tears flow again. My face must have been a mess, but the tears left no stain where they dropped onto the princess's dress. I meekly refastened the griffin around my neck, and it settled comfortably into the hollow of my throat.

I knew he was there, standing uncertainly before my door, several minutes before he said, tentatively: "Beauty? Is something wrong?" I was usually changed and downstairs again in less than half the time I had spent sitting on the floor tonight.

"They're forcing me to wear a dress I don't like," I said sulkily, from the floor. "I mean, it won't come off."

"Forcing you? Why?"

"I haven't the faintest idea!" I shouted, and pulled off a few bracelets and hurled them at the fireplace. They half-turned and threw themselves back at me, and over my wrists.

"That's very odd," he said through the door. After a pause, he added, "What's wrong with it?"

"I don't like it," I said sullenly.

"Er—may I see?"

"Of course not!" I shouted again. "If I didn't mind your seeing it, why am I staying in my room? Who else is there to see me?"

"You care how I see you?" he said; his voice was muffled by the door, and I could be sure of only the astonishment.

"Well, I won't wear it," I said, avoiding the question.

There was a pause and then a roar that made me cower down where I sat and clap my hands over my ears; but I realized in a moment that it wasn't the sort of roar I could protect myself from that way. I couldn't catch the words. Whatever it was, I found myself hauled to my feet and tumbled in several directions at once; and when I emerged again, breathless, the fairy dress was gone. So, my sixth sense told me, were Lydia and Bessie. I was wearing a dress of an indeterminate color somewhere between beige and grey; the only decoration was a white yoke, and plain white cuffs on the long straight sleeves. The high round collar reached nearly to my chin. I laughed, and went over to open the door. As I moved, I felt something around my neck; I put my hand up. It was the griffin.

I opened the door, and the Beast looked at me gravely. "I fear that they are angry with you," he said.

"Yes, I think you're right," I said cheerfully. "What did you say to them? Whatever it was, it nearly deafened me. If deafened is the word."

"Did you hear that? I'm sorry. I'll be more careful in the future."

"That's all right," I said. "It produced the desired result."

"Shall we go down then?" he said. He turned, and waved me towards the staircase.

I looked at him a moment. "Aren't you going to offer me your arm?" I said.

There was a silence, while we stared at one another, as if every candle, every tile in the mosaic floor and colored thread in the tapestries, had caught its breath and was holding it as it watched. The Beast walked the few paces back to me, turned, and offered me his arm. I laid my hand on it, and we walked downstairs.

4

Summer turned gradually, peacefully, to autumn. I had been in the Beast's castle for over six months. I was no nearer the answer to the riddle of the magic that Lydia and Bessie hinted was laid on the Beast and his estate; nor did my sixth sense develop any further. Or at least—I didn't think so. I found I could read more of the books in the library with comprehension; if I stopped and tried deliberately to envision, say, a motorcar, I managed only a headache, and my reading was spoiled. But if once I slipped into an author's world, nothing in it disturbed me, and I could slip out of it again when I closed the book. But perhaps there was nothing really mysterious in that. I had accepted Cassandra and Medea, and Paris's choice among three goddesses as the reason for the Trojan War, and other improbables long before I read about steam-engines and telephones; I had accepted my life in this castle, for example. The principle was probably the same.

I continued to listen to Lydia and Bessie's conversations without acknowledging that I could hear them, but I learned nothing that was useful. I had trouble, sometimes, when I inadvertently made comments I shouldn't have been able to make. But Lydia was straightforward and trusting and never—I think—suspected. Bessie may have; she was the quieter of the two, and I didn't know her as well; and she said nothing that would indicate one way or another. Perhaps the Beast had warned them. I didn't see the princess's dress again, nor the convent schoolgirl's dress, and neither of them referred to that incident; although, once or twice, Lydia said with meaning during minor squabbles: "Now we *know* how stubborn she can be." Whereupon I won.

I occasionally heard other things talking to one another, especially the plates and trays and glasses on the grand dinner table; but they spoke in a language that I had never learned. I understood a phrase, sometimes, by not listening: It was usually something like "Here you, move over;" or "I won't have this, it's *my* turn," that would spill into my mind. But mostly I heard nothing more than echoes behind the clink of silver and crystal. This, with Lydia and Bessie, served to make me feel far less lonely; and the castle never again seemed as immense and solitary as it once had after I'd heard, once or twice, "Hsst—wake up, you," and seen a startled candle burst into flame.

And I always knew where the Beast was. If he was at a good distance, I could ignore him. If he was nearby, it was like listening to the soughing of wind through tall trees—it was there, and while I could choose not to pay attention to it, I couldn't pretend it didn't exist. Usually this latter situation prevailed. "Beast," I said, exasperated, about a week after the night I'd fainted, "do you always lurk like this?"

"I like to watch you," he said. "Does it disturb you?"

"Oh—well," I said, off balance. "I suppose not."

When I looked out over the forest from my bedroom window there was a rosy flush of autumn leaves among the evergreens, and I began to wear a cloak again on the afternoon rides. I thought of my family as little as possible, putting them out of my head, and resisting any attempts to return to them.

Although I had almost contrived to forget what the Beast had said that night many weeks ago, just before I fainted, it was nonetheless the reason that I had since then chosen never to think about the future. When I did remember my family—and I dreamed of them very often, nor were they ever far from my conscious mind, even if I would not entertain them there—I thought of them as I had left them. I avoided thinking about how much the babies must have grown, and whether Ger and Father had had time to build the extra room on the house as they had planned. I never allowed myself to think about seeing them again. And much deeper than all of this in my mind, where I probably couldn't have reached it even if I had wanted to, was the thought that I couldn't leave my Beast now even if the opportunity were offered. I still wanted to visit my family, and I missed them desperately; but not if leaving this world to return to theirs meant that I could not come back here. But I was only dimly aware of the smallest part of this. Consciously I understood only that to save myself needless pain I must not think about my life before I had come to live in the castle.

And every night before I left him in the dining hall the Beast asked, "Beauty, will you marry me?" And every night I closed my eyes, my heart, and my mind, and replied, "No, Beast."

This magic land was not entirely free of the lashing storms of autumn. In October there was a day heavy and grey with foreboding, and that night I had difficulty sleeping, as the clouds crept lower and lower, and hung themselves balefully around the castle's high towers. It was past midnight when the rain finally broke through; but even then it was nearly dawn when I fell uneasily asleep, and dreamed. I dreamed of my family, as I often did, but never before had I dreamed of them with such vividness.

They were eating breakfast—I could even smell the thick porridge as Grace spooned it into bowls. Everyone sat around the kitchen table, and there were two conversations going on at once. Ger and Father were having a friendly argument over the cutting of floorboards; Hope was telling Grace that Melinda had managed to find some thread from her own large supply that would just match the green cotton she wanted to make into a dress. Grace set the full bowls around while Hope cut bread, and Father passed the plate of fried ham. The babies were wielding spoons, sort of; Richard was mashing his bit of bread into the bottom of his bowl with the back of his spoon, to the accompaniment of much interesting splashing. Mercy tried to help, till their mother prevented her, and also rearranged her son's hold on his spoon. "It's nice to have the cool weather back," said Grace; "cooking over the fire in the middle of summer exhausts me."

"Yes, I like fall," said Hope, "after harvest, when everyone has the first bit of breathing space since spring sowing. That was quite a storm we had last night, though, wasn't it? But this morning is fair; it must have blown itself out."

"It's funny, the way the roses never seem to lose their petals, even with the wind," murmured Grace, and she and Hope glanced towards a vase on the table that held a dozen gold and red and white roses. "Or the way they never grow over the windows," said Hope. "They've never been pruned, have they?" Grace shook her head.

Ger glanced over at them. "Pruned?" he inquired.

"The roses. Beauty's roses," said Grace. "They never need pruning. And they don't seem to care about storms that take the heads off all the other flowers within miles of here."

"And after they're cut, they live a month to the day, looking as if they had just been brought inside, and then they die in a night," said Hope.

Ger smiled and shrugged. "It's a good omen, don't you think? The flowers so beautiful and all? I wonder if they'll bloom all through the winter? That'll make the townspeople talk."

"I think they'll always bloom," said Father. "Summer or winter."

Ger looked at him. "Did you dream about her last night?"

"Yes." He paused. "She was riding Greatheart towards the castle. She was wearing a long blue habit, and a cloak that billowed out behind her. She waved at someone I couldn't see. She looked happy." He shook his head. "I dream about her—often, as you know. And I've noticed—oh, just recently it's occurred to me—she's changed. Changing. First I thought, I'm forgetting her, and it made me very unhappy. But it's not that. She's *changing*. My dreams are as vivid as ever, but the Beauty I see is different."

"How?" asked Grace.

"I don't know. I wish I did. I wish I knew where the dreams come from—whether I dream truly."

"I think you do," said Hope. "I believe you do. It's like the roses; they comfort us."

Father smiled. "I like to think that too."

Then Mercy said in a clear thin treble: "When is Beauty coming home?"

Her words were like a rock in a quiet pool that I, the dreamer, was looking into: I saw only the beginnings of wonder, surprise, and a little fear in the faces of the rest of the family before the image was shattered, and my sleep with it. My first coherent thought, as I awoke, was: I was wearing the blue habit yesterday; I saw the Beast, and waved at him, as we cantered back towards the castle.

Dawn came clear and pale through my window. The storm was blown away and the sky was blue and cloudless.

I was still tired; I nodded over my teacup, and walked slowly downstairs and out into the garden.

"Good morning, Beauty," said the Beast.

"Good morning," I returned, and yawned. "I'm sorry. The storm kept me awake most of the night." I was tired, and didn't mean to add: "And I had an upsetting dream just before I woke up," and I yawned again, and then realized what I'd said.

"What was it?" he asked.

"It's not important," I mumbled. We had been walking towards the stable as we spoke, and I went inside to let Greatheart out. He ambled through the door, pricked his ears at the Beast, and wandered off in search of grass.

The meadows were still wet from last night's rain; I was wearing boots, but the hem of my dress was soon soaked through.

After several minutes' silence, the Beast said: "Was it about your family?"

I opened my mouth to deny it, and changed my mind. I nodded, looking down and kicking at a daisy. It shook itself free of raindrops that the sunlight turned into a halo. "Must you read my mind?" I said.

"I can't," said the Beast. "But in this case your face is transparent enough."

"I dream about them a lot," I said, "but it was different this time. It was like watching them—it was as if I were really in the room, except they couldn't see me. I could see the knots in the wood of the table—not because I remembered them, but because I saw them. Ger had a bandage wrapped around one thumb. I recognized the shirt Father was wearing, but it had a new patch on one shoulder. I *saw* them."

The Beast nodded. "Did you hear them too?"

"Yes," I said slowly. "They—they were talking about me. And the roses. My father said he had dreamed about me—I was riding towards the castle, I was wearing my blue habit, and I looked happy. He said he wished he knew if he dreamed truly; and Hope said she was sure he did, that the dreams and the roses were to comfort them."

"She's right," said the Beast.

"How do you know?" I asked.

"The roses are mine," said the Beast. "And I send the dreams."

I stared at him.

"He dreams about you nearly every night, and tells the rest of your family about it the next day. It does comfort them, I think. I am careful not to let him see me."

"How do you know? Can you see them?" I said, still staring.

He looked away. "Yes; I can see them."

"May I?"

He looked at me, and his eyes were unhappy. "I will show you, if you wish it."

"Please," I said. "Oh, please show me."

I put Greatheart away, and the Beast took me back inside the castle, up stairs and down hallways and up more stairs to the room I had found him in on the very first night. He closed the curtains and the door, and I noticed that the small table that stood behind the Beast's armchair glittered strangely. He went over to it and peered at it;

then he picked up a glass that stood on the mantelpiece, and said a few words as he poured a little of its contents onto the tabletop. He replaced the glass and said to me, "Come here, stand by me."

I could see that on the table a thick plate of what looked like pale nephrite lay. The glitter had died, and there was a cloudy grey swirling like harbour water just after the turn of the tide. It cleared slowly.

I saw my sisters in the parlour. Grace was sitting, head in hands, and Hope stood in front of her, hands on Grace's shoulders. "What's wrong, dearest?" she said. "What's wrong?" Morning sunlight streamed in the window, and I heard Ger's laugh, faintly, from the shop. "Is it something about Mr. Lawrey? I just saw him leaving."

Grace nodded slowly, and spoke into her hands. "He wants to marry me."

Hope knelt down and pulled Grace's hands away from her face, and they looked at one another. "He has asked you?"

"Not quite. He's much too proper—you know. But his hints—and he just told me that he wants to 'speak' to Father. What else could he mean?"

"Of course," said Hope. "We've suspected all summer that this was coming. Father will be pleased—he thinks

Mr. Lawrey is a very good sort of young man. It'll be all right. You'll make a lovely minister's wife, you're so good and patient."

Grace's eyes filled with tears. "No," she whispered. "I can't." The tears spilled over and ran down her pale face. Hope reached out and touched her sister's wet cheek with her hand. Her voice was a whisper too. "You're not still thinking of Robbie, are you?"

Grace nodded. "I can't help it," she said through her tears. "We never *knew*. And I don't love Pat Lawrey—I still love Robbie. I can't seem to think of anyone else. I can't even try to. Have I been terribly unfair to Mr. Lawrey?"

"No," said Hope, as if she weren't quite sure. "No, don't worry about that. But Father will encourage him, you know, and he'll start courting you in earnest. Oh, my dear, you must try to put Robbie out of your mind. You can't waste your life like this. It's been six years."

"I know," said Grace. "Do you think I've forgotten a day of it? But it's no use."

"Try," said Hope. "Please. Mr. Lawrey loves you and would be good to you. You needn't love him as you did Robbie." Hope's voice was unsteady and she had begun to weep also. "Just be good to him—time and his love for you will do the rest. I'm sure of it. Please, Grace."

Grace looked at her like a lost child. "Must I? Is this the only way left to me?"

"Yes," said Hope. "Trust me. It's for your own good—I know it. And it would please Father so much. You know how he worries about you."

"Yes." Grace bowed her head. "Very well; I will do as you say," she whispered.

The mist gathered around the picture again, and then across it, and my sisters disappeared. "Oh, poor Grace," I said, "poor Grace. I wonder what did happen to Robbie?"

As I spoke, the mist disappeared like a fog before a high wind, and a man stepped down from a ship's side to the dock. There was a brisk wind blowing across a harbour I knew well: I had grown up on it and beside it. I could see one of the warehouses that used to belong to Father. It had had a new addition built onto it, and it was freshly painted. The ship the man left was two-masted, but the second mast had been snapped off a third of its length from the deck, and a spar lashed to the stump. The rest of the ship was sadly battered also; there were gaps in her railing, hasty patches on her sides and her deck; most of the forward cabin had been torn away, and canvas sheeting turned the remains into a sort of tent. The men who manned her were ragged and hollow-eyed, nor were there many of them; but they stood to attention with a pride that showed in their faces and in their bearing. Several men from the shore came hurrying up to the one who had just stepped off the ship. They made a curious contrast: These men were stout and healthy, and well-dressed. The man they confronted was much taller than they, but thin and pale as if he had been very ill recently and had not yet fully recovered. His black hair was streaked with white.

"Please excuse me, masters," he said; "we lost both our skiffs over the side during storms. I thought it would be best to tie up at the dock rather than trust to luck in hailing another ship in the harbour. You see," he added with a grin, "I'm afraid we've lost our anchor also, and the old tub is leaking so fast that I thought it would be well that my men be near enough to leap ashore when the time comes. We're not fit for much swimming."

I recognized the grin when I hadn't recognized the man. It was Robbie.

"But who are you, sir?" said one of the men who approached him.

"My name is Robert Tucker, and my ship—what's left of her—is the *White Raven*. I sail—or I used to—for Roderick Huston. I set out six years ago with three other ships: the *Stalwart,* the *Windfleet,* and the *Fortune's Chance.* I'm afraid we ran into rather more trouble than we were expecting." I couldn't see the faces of the men he was talking to. One young lad, dressed like an office boy, detached himself from the group and ran off to spread the news. After a pause, Robbie went on: "Can you tell me what's become of the other three? We lost track of them entirely, four years ago, during a storm— the first storm," he said wryly. "And where might I find Mr. Huston? Things have changed, I see, since we've been gone," and he nodded towards the warehouse I had noticed. "He must have written us off long since. We've not been anywhere that we could well send a message from. I tried, once or twice, but I don't suppose they ever arrived."

And then the mist obliterated the picture once again, and I found myself staring at the top of a table in a dark room in the Beast's castle. "Robbie," I said. "He's come home—he's alive! And Grace doesn't know—oh dear—Beast," I said, turning to him, "is what I'm seeing happening now? Has Robbie only just docked? And Grace only just had her conversation with Hope?"

The Beast nodded.

"Then it's not too late," I said. "Yet. Oh dear. If

Robbie sets out for Blue Hill today it'll take him nearly two months—and he wouldn't, besides: He'll stay and see to the ship, and his men. And he's not well—you can see that just by looking at him. I wonder if he'll even send a message. You can never tell with these desperately honour-bound people; he may think he has to put it off for some reason. Oh *dear*," I said. I walked away from the table, and paced up and down the room several times. The Beast wiped a cloth carefully over the table and then sat down in the big chair near it, but I was preoccupied and paid him little attention. "Grace must be told. If she gets herself engaged to that young minister—if she even feels that she's encouraged him to believe that she would accept his suit—she'll go through with it. She'll feel she must, Robbie or no Robbie.

"Beast—could you send her a dream—telling her about Robbie?"

He shifted in his chair. "I could try, but I doubt that I would be successful. And even if I were, she would not believe it."

"Why? Father believes."

"Yes, but he wants to—and there are the roses that remind him that there is some magic at work. Grace often dreams that Robbie is safely home. She knows that the dreams are wraiths of her own love, and so she has trained herself not to believe. She would not believe any dream I sent. And—well—both your sisters' minds are strongly pragmatic; I'm not sure I could send them anything at all. Your father is different—so is Ger, for that matter; so is Mercy. But neither your father nor Ger would mention dreaming of Robbie, you know, to save your sister pain; and Mercy is too young."

I paused in my pacing. "You know a great deal about my family."

"I have watched them many hours, since your father rode home alone. They have grown very dear to me, perhaps for your sake; and I have watched to see that they were well."

"Then let me go home—just for a day—an hour—to tell Grace. She mustn't marry Lawrey—she'll be miserable for the rest of her life, after she finds out that her heart was right about Robbie. And then they'll know too that I'm all right, that I'm happy here, that they needn't worry about me anymore. And then I'll come back. And I'll never ask to leave again. Please, Beast. Please." I knelt down in front of him and put my hands on his knees. The room was still dark, the curtains unopened, and his face was hidden in the darker shadows of the wing chair; all I could see was a glitter of eyes. There was a long silence, while I could hear nothing but the quick heave of my own breathing.

"I can deny you nothing," he said at last, "if you truly want it. Even if it should cost me my life." He took a deep breath; it seemed that he would suck in all the air in the room. "Go home, then. I can give you a week." He leaned forwards. There was a bowl of roses on a what-not at his elbow; he lifted out a great red one, like the one Father had brought home nearly eight months ago. "Take this." I took it, the stem still wet, cool against my fingers. "For a week it will remain fresh and blooming, as it is now; but at the end of the week it will droop and die. You will know then that your faithful Beast is dying too. For I cannot live without you, Beauty."

I looked at him, appalled, and with a little gasp and gulp I said: "Can you not send me as you send dreams? It would be much swifter. And—and you would know when to bring me back, before—anything happened."

"I could," he said. "But you must take Greatheart with you, and I cannot send him thus, as I have already told you; it would drive him mad."

"He could stay here, with you," I said.

"No; he suffers me only for love of you. You must

take him with you. If you leave at once, you will be home in time for supper."

Those words, "home in time for supper," filled my whole world and echoed in every part of my head, and I spared no further thought for any of my scruples at leaving the poor Beast. All the longing to see my family that I had suppressed so urgently over the last few months surged and poured into me till I could scarcely breathe. I stood up, looking through the thick walls of the castle to a little house on the far side of the enchanted forest.

"Wear your ring," said the Beast, "and remember me."

I laughed, and my voice was shrill with excitement. "I couldn't forget you, dear Beast," I said, and bent down. His hands lay, fingers curled a little upwards, on his knees; I kissed the right palm, and looked into the shadows for a moment, where his eyes watched me. The glitter of them was strangely bright, as if reflected by tears; but that must have been the blur in my own vision. As I turned away, I saw his right hand close slowly.

I ran to my room, down a hallway and around the first corner, pulled out a silk scarf, and bundled a few things into it; then a loaf of bread from breakfast and a few oranges into another scarf, and knotted them hastily together. It did not occur to me, that day, to wonder why breakfast had not yet been cleared away. I grabbed my cloak and bolted downstairs. Greatheart knew at once that something was up. I fastened the rose to his headstall as I had done with another rose, when we had first followed the path that we were about to retrace. I pushed my small bundles into the saddlebags, and mounted; Greatheart had thundered into a canter before I was settled in the saddle. I grabbed the reins.

The silver gate winked at us across the meadows; we were beside it, it seemed, before I had my feet in the stirrups. But when I looked back, the castle was far away, the gardens only a memory outlined in delicate green. I pulled Greatheart to a halt for a moment, a strange and unexpectedly queasy moment for me; but I thought, Nonsense; I'll be back in a week. We jogged through the gate, and it swung silently shut behind us.

I had no idea of direction, hadn't thought to ask the Beast before I left, but Greatheart jogged steadily along the carriage-road as if he knew where he was going. I remembered that the road ran out within a few miles of the grey gates; but the dark afternoon shadows lengthened across the sand-colored road, and it still showed no sign of ending. I had a queer, sixth-sense feeling that just beyond the first shadow up ahead that I couldn't see through, the road ended, but had unrolled as far as the next shadow by the time we had reached the first. Greatheart trotted tirelessly; I knew that we still had a long way to go, and we should reserve our strength, but when I slackened the reins, the horse leaped forwards into a gallop. I let him run, the sun sparkling in his pale mane as it lifted and fell with the motion, the pale road unfolding just beyond the edge of sight.

We stopped once, and I slacked the girths and fed Greatheart pieces of bread and orange, but we were both eager to go on. I tried to make him walk, but he fretted so that I told myself that he was wasting more energy than if I let him jog; so we jogged.

The sun sank beyond our sight, and twilight crept out from behind the trees and spread across our way; the road glimmered faintly. Then something else, a golden glimmer, showed among the trees for a moment and was gone. Then it showed again. It might be lamplight from a house. I leaned forwards and Greatheart broke into a gallop again, and galloped till the reins were slippery with sweat; and then we burst through the border of the trees, and we were in the meadow behind the house, lamplight gleaming through the kitchen window, goldedging the roses that hung near it, and laying down a little golden carpet on the grass verge between the back door and the kitchen garden. Greatheart plunged to a stop, then threw his head out and neighed like a warhorse. There was a moment of dreadful silence, then the back door flew open, and Hope said, "It *is* Greatheart!" and I slid out of the saddle and ran to the door. By the time I got there, everyone else had come outside, and we laughed and hugged one another, and Greatheart, who had followed me for his share of the attention, was petted and kissed, and most if not all of us were crying.

The babies, left alone in the kitchen, had made their way to the door and were looking curiously at the confusion outside. Mercy slid down the two steps to the ground and stood, precariously, clutching one of the posts of the chicken-wire fence that protected the garden from the little creatures that never came out of the enchanted forest. "Mercy," said her grandfather, after the initial uproar had subsided, "do you remember Beauty?" "No," she replied, but when I walked over to her she smiled at me and held up her arms. I picked her up, while the more timid Richard made a dash from the door and wrapped himself in his mother's skirts.

"Come in, come in," said Father. "You must tell us everything."

"Wait, I have to put Greatheart away—is there space for him?"

"We'll make space," said Ger.

"I'll set another place at the table," said Grace. "We're just sitting down to dinner." All our voices sounded strange, breathless, and creaky; I found it difficult to think clearly. Grace and Hope and Richard went back inside the house while the rest of us went out to the stable. "Would Mercy like a ride?" I said, with laudable presence of mind; my own earliest memories were of wanting to sit on horses. "Try her," said Ger. "She and Richard are old friends with Odysseus now." Mercy was arranged on Greatheart's saddle and held by the leg from both sides, and we safely navigated the few steps to the stable. Ger went inside to light a lantern. "Big" was Mercy's comment when she was lifted down.

Besides Odysseus's brown blazed face, there was a new chestnut face that looked over Greatheart's old stall door. "Cider," said Ger. "Five years old; a nice little mare. I hope they'll get along. We can tie Greatheart in a corner, here. There's plenty of hay." I pulled off the saddle. My head was ringing.

"Hurry up, can't you?" begged Father, who was holding Mercy. "I mustn't ask you anything till we go back

inside and join the girls and the suspense is killing me."
Just then Hope appeared in the doorway. "Are you going
to stay here all night? We'll die of suspense, and the food
will get cold, in that order." Ger took my saddle-bags, and
we walked back, I with an arm each around Hope and my
father. "I don't believe it yet," I said. "Neither do we,"
said Hope, and hugged me again.

It wasn't until we were inside the house and in
the light that something that had been bothering me
obscurely struck me with full force. I looked at Hope,
who was still standing near me: "You've *shrunk*," I
squeaked. I was looking down at her, and seven months
ago I had looked up, several inches. Hope laughed; "My
dear, you've grown!" Grace, the taller of the two, came
to stand next to me; I was even an inch or so taller than
she. "There! We always told you you'd grow; you were
just too impatient, and wouldn't believe us," she said,
smiling.

"Seven inches in seven months isn't bad," said Ger. "I
hope this trend will not continue too much longer."

"Oh, stop it, spoilsport," Hope said. "And look at the
roses in your cheeks!" she said to me. "Enchantments
agree with you. I've never seen you look prettier."

I grinned. "That's not saying much, little sister."

"Now, children," said Grace mock-seriously. "No fighting. Let's eat."

"Do we have to wait till after dinner to hear your story?" said Father plaintively. "At least tell us: Are you home for good and ever now?"

"No," I said, as gently as I could. "I'm afraid not. It's just a visit." In the joy of coming home the real reason for my visit had been brushed aside and buried; now I recalled it. I cast a quick glance at Grace, who was smiling at me. "I'll tell you all about it after dinner," I said. "I'm hungry. . . . You could tell me about what's been happening here since I've been gone. It seems like years. I half-expect to see the babies all grown up."

"Not yet," said Hope, rescuing Mercy's cup just before she knocked it on the floor.

It had been a good year for them, happy—except for the loss of the youngest daughter—and certainly prosperous. Ger's reputation had spread till he had more work than he could do. "I could just about keep abreast of it—I hate turning people away, particularly if they've come from a distance—but then, a month ago, Ferdy was called away. He'd become nearly indispensable to me in those six months; but an uncle in Goose Landing was badly hurt by a falling log, and they needed somebody to help look after the farm; their children are all very young. So Ferdy went, and I'm afraid we won't be getting him back. I have Melinda's oldest boy working for me now; he's a little young, but he's doing well. But it'll take time for him to learn everything he needs—I need him—to know."

"And what's suffering for it worst is the extra room we're trying to build on the house," said Father. "We'd hoped to have it finished by winter, but we won't now." Father's carpentry business had improved to the point where he could specialize in what he could build at home, in the shop. "I'm too old to crawl around on other people's roofs," he said, "and I like working at home. Beds and trunks and cradles, and chairs and tables, and the occasional wagon or cart, mostly. And some repairs. I seem to make a terrible lot of wheels. I get a little fancy work now and then—that's what I like best—scrollwork on a desk, carved legs on a table."

"Nothing much new from us," said Hope. "I run after the babies, and Grace runs after me. This year's cider turned out really well—even better than Melinda's, if you can believe it—we'll all have some, after dinner."

"That's where the new mare gets her name, as you might expect," said Ger. "We were all feeling so smug about it, and then this horse comes along—we bought her from Dick Johnson, you remember him?—with a coat of just the right color."

"We couldn't resist," said Hope.

"Yes," said Ger. "And I was very unfairly accused of buying her for her color." Hope laughed. "You may not have noticed," he continued, "but we have a cow byre now too, built onto the other wall of the stable. Rosie has the rabbits and chickens to keep her company. Odysseus doesn't seem to like cows for some reason, so we had to build her her own stable."

"You're wealthy," I said admiringly.

"You haven't seen the new carpet in the parlour yet, either," added Grace.

"Not so wealthy as you," said Hope, "judging from that wonderful dress you're wearing." I hadn't bothered to change that morning, at the castle, into riding clothes; the dress I was wearing was rich and heavy, and quite ridiculous for traveling. "Come on now," Hope continued, "we're all finished eating. What's happened to you?"

"The Beast is kind to you, just as he promised?" said Father.

"Yes, Papa," I said, and paused. Pictures of the gardens, the castle, the incredible library, and the Beast himself crowded into my mind. "I don't know where to begin."

"Begin in the middle and work outwards," said Hope. "Don't be stuffy."

"All right," I said. So I told them about Lydia and Bessie, and the candles that lit themselves, and the way my room was always down a short hallway and around a corner from wherever I was as soon as I felt lost. I told them about how big and grand the castle was, and the enormous table where I ate dinner every night, where I could have anything I pleased by asking for it, and the way the serving trays jostled one another in their enthusiasm to decant their contents onto my plate. I told them about the little friendly birds at my bird-feeder. I told them about the huge library, with more books in it than I could ever begin to read.

"I didn't think there were that many books in the world," Grace said drily. I smiled and shrugged. I found that I couldn't quite say to them: "Well, you see, most of the books don't exist yet." I found that there was quite a lot that I skipped over because I didn't feel that I could explain it.

My greatest difficulty was the Beast himself. I couldn't leave him out of my narrative, yet I had tremendous trouble bringing him into it; and when I did mention him I found myself pleading in his defense. The ogre my father had met was the Beast they all believed in; and while they were relieved to hear that he was "good" to me I didn't seem to be able to tell them how good and kind he really was. I stumbled over explanations of how fond I had come to be of him, and what a good friend I found him. It seemed disloyal, somehow. It was he who had cruelly taken me away from my family in the first place; how could they or I forgive him that? How could I make excuses? I couldn't tell them that I—loved him. This thought came to me with an unpleasant jolt. Loved him?

I fell silent and looked at the fire. I was holding a cup of warm spiced cider; they were right, it was very good. It was strange to cope with dishes that lay where you set them, and didn't jump up and hurry over to you if you beckoned. And the food was very plain, but I didn't mind that; what I did mind was a sense that I no longer belonged here, in this warm golden kitchen. You're only just home, I told myself. It's been a long time; of course you've accustomed yourself to a different life. You've had to. Relax.

"How long can you stay?" asked Hope. "You said that you have to go back."

I nodded. The warmth of the kitchen seemed to retreat from me, leave me isolated. I looked around at the faces of my family. "Yes. I'm here for—for just a week."

"A *week*?" Father said. "Only a week? That's all?"

"Surely you'll come back again?" said Grace.

I was a traitor, questioned pitilessly by a beloved enemy. I twisted my hands in my lap; the cider tasted bitter. "Well—no," I said, and my words dropped like knives in the silence. There was a sharp edge to the firelight I hadn't noticed before, staining the corners with blood. "I—I promised I wouldn't ask to leave again." What can I tell them? I thought desperately. The Beast had said, "I cannot live without you." They wouldn't understand that I must go back.

"Forever?" said Hope, and her voice disappeared on the last syllable.

"Why did he let you go at all?" Father said angrily.

This wasn't the time to tell them. "Just to—well, to let you know I'm all right," I said lamely, "so you wouldn't have to worry about me anymore."

"Worry—but we love you," he said. "We can't help worrying if we never see you."

"Well—the dreams you have about me"—I faltered—"they're true. They help, don't they?"

"How do you know about that?" demanded Father.

"The Beast sends them. He told me."

"He sends dreams—very kind of him, I'm sure—but he keeps you. What kind of a bargain is that? Oh, that I had never seen his castle, nor accepted his lying hospitality!"

"Oh, please, Father," I said, "don't be angry. You don't understand. I miss you all, of course, but I don't mind that much anymore—I mean, I'd rather be here, of course, but . . ." I couldn't think how to go on.

"Understand? Understand what?"

"The Beast is lonely too," I said desperately, and there was an aghast silence.

"You can have—sympathy—for this monster, after what he's done to you?" said Father at last. I nodded unhappily, and there was more astonished silence.

"All right," said Ger, in the tone of one trying very hard to be reasonable. "I don't understand what's going on, but we know this much: There's magic mixed up in all of this—these invisible servants you talk about, and so on—and none of us can understand magic. I guess what you're trying to tell us now, Beauty, is that the Beast you know is not the same monster that your father met. Is that right?"

I smiled with an effort. "It will do." And I added with unforced gratitude: "Thanks."

Richard and Mercy had fallen asleep in their chairs, and Grace and Hope picked them up to carry them to bed. "It's a funny thing," said Hope, brushing a curl off Mercy's forehead. "She said her first sentence just this morning, at breakfast. She said: 'When is Beauty coming home?'" And a tear crept down Hope's cheek.

We resettled ourselves in the parlour while the babies were put to bed; none of the rest of us said anything till Grace and Hope returned, bringing with them a jug of cider and a plate of gingerbread. We all had our glasses refilled; but then the silence seeped back and filled the room so closely that it was difficult to see through, like flame. Hope stirred restlessly and sighed, then reached over to pluck at a fold of my long skirt and rub it between her fingers. "You're dressed like a queen," she said. "I suppose you have wardrobes full of clothing like this?"

"Oh, more or less," I said, embarrassed, although there was nothing in Hope's face but gentle curiosity; and it was slowly being borne in on me that my stories about the castle and my life there had little reality for my family. They listened with interest to what I told—or tried to tell—them, but it was for my sake, not for the sake of the tale. I could not say if this was my fault or theirs, or the fault of the worlds we lived in. The only thing they had understood was that I would be leaving them again, to return to a fantastic destiny; and I began to see how horrible this must appear to them. And I also began to sense that there was little I could do to help them.

I smiled at Hope, as she looked pleadingly at me, and in answer to her look I said: "A lot of them are too fancy for me, and I won't wear them. I wish I'd thought to bring you some of them; they'd look lovely on you two." I thought of the silvery, gauzy dress I had refused to wear a few weeks ago.

My commonplace words cleared the air. "From the weight of your saddle-bags I thought you brought half the castle with you," Ger said cheerfully.

"I—what?" I said. "Where are they?" Ger pointed to the table in a corner of the room, and I walked over to them. There was certainly more in them than I had put there. I threw back the flap of the first, and a dull gold brocade with tiny rubies sewed on it looked up at me. "Thank you, Beast," I said under my breath; and I had a sudden, dizzy, involuntary glimpse of him leaning over the far-seeing glass in the dark room in the castle. It was night; the curtains behind him where he stood were open, and I could see a few stars. There was a fire burning in the fireplace, turning the chestnut-colored velvet he wore to a ruddier hue. Then the vision faded. I had both hands laid flat on the table in front of me, and I shook my head to clear it. "Are you all right?" said Father. "Yes, of course," I said. Apparently my new ways of seeing rested uneasily in my old world. Then I knew where I was again, and I was looking at golden brocade.

I pulled it out. It was a ball-dress, with satin ribbons woven into the bodice, and rubies alternating with pearls. "This must be yours," I said, and tossed it at Grace. She reached a hand out for it only at the last minute, and yards and yards of skirt cascaded across her shoulders and lap. There were shoes that matched the dress, tall ruby-studded combs for her hair, and ropes of rubies to wind around her throat.

Underneath all this was a jade-green dress, hemmed with emeralds, for Hope; then two long embroidered cloaks and hoods, and soft leather gloves lined with white fur. Underneath these were fine clothes for Father and Ger; and in a little soft satchel at the back where I almost overlooked it were dresses and caps for the babies, little pearl and sapphire pins, and tiny blankets of the finest wool.

The parlour glittered like a king's treasure house. I had taken more out of that saddle-bag than could ever have fit into it in the first place; and there was the second saddle-bag, still full, that I had not yet touched. Hope, with a string of emeralds around her neck and a green shawl over one arm, the silken fringe trailing to her feet, picked up one of the little dresses I had laid on the table, and sighed. "I've wanted to be able to dress the twins in something really fine; but it's impractical when they grow so fast—and these are far more beautiful than I was dreaming of. I don't know, indeed, what we're going to do with all this—but I love just looking at it. Thank you, Beauty dear," and she kissed me.

"I want no presents from the Beast," said Father. "Is he trying to buy us off? Let him take his rich gifts back, and leave us our girl."

"Please, Father," I said. "Think of them as presents from me. I'd like you to keep them, and think of me." Father dropped his eyes, and reluctantly put out a hand and stroked the fur collar of his new jacket.

Ger sighed. "I still don't understand—and I don't like not understanding. It makes me feel like a child again, with my mother telling me bogey stories. But I will do as you say—and, since it pleases you—" He picked up his cap, and twirled it on one finger. "Your Beast must be very fond of you, to be so kind to your family." Father snorted, but said nothing. "Thank you both," Ger said, and he kissed me too. "I've always wondered what it would be like to dress like a lord; here's my opportunity." He put the hat on backwards, and pulled it low on his forehead so that the feather tickled his chin. "I feel different already," he said, blowing at the feather, and Hope laughed. "You look different."

"Yes, I will cause quite a stir wearing this hat and white satin breeches to shoe horses. It's a pity I didn't ask for a new pair of bellows to be thrown in with this deal. The price of the feather alone would probably buy them." He put the hat on straight, and Hope picked up his cloak and put it around his shoulders, and arranged the golden chain and clasps. Ger stood still while she fussed over him, with a bit of a smile pulling at his mouth. We looked at him as Hope stepped back. He still looked like Ger as we all knew him, but he was different too; you could imagine this Ger commanding armies. With his heavy hair pushed back under the cap, you noticed the height and breadth of his forehead, and the straight proud lines of his eyebrows and mouth.

"I feel silly," he said. "Don't stare at me so"; and he

took the cap off, and the cloak, and dwindled again to Hope's husband and the finest blacksmith in a half dozen towns.

"You looked like a lord," said Hope, smiling.

"Fond wife," he replied, putting an arm around her waist.

Grace had left her chair, the gold dress heaped over the back of it and spilling across the seat, to light several candles and lamps to augment the firelight. "If we're going to be grand, we should see what we're doing," she said, and as she passed me, she kissed me and whispered in my ear: "Thank you, dear heart. I don't care that I can't wear it; I shall look at it every night, and think of you. I'll even try and think kindly of your dreadful Beast." I smiled.

Father stood up and smiled at me too, but it was a sad smile. "Very well, my dear, you win the day—as you seem always to do. As Ger says, I don't understand; but there's magic at work, so—well, I'll do what you say, and try to be glad of what we have—of what you tell us. We shan't let you out of our sight for the week, you know."

I nodded. "I hope not."

We all went to bed shortly after this. I realized that I still hadn't told Grace about Robbie. "Tomorrow," I thought. "Tonight would have been too soon, too much. But I mustn't put it off anymore." My attic looked just as I remembered it, only somewhat cleaner; Grace kept it much better than I ever had. The sheets on the bed were fresh and clean, not stiff and musty with six months' neglect, and the bed was made up very neatly, which was not at all how I had left it. I sat on the trunk, under the window, and stared out across the meadow and into the forest.

My thoughts went back to the evening just past, of the scene around the parlour fire, when I had tried to plead for my Beast against my family's animosity. I knew now what it was that had happened. I couldn't tell them that here, at home with them again, I had learned what I had successfully ignored these last weeks at the castle: that I had come to love him. They were no less dear to me, but he was dearer yet. I thought of the enchantment that I didn't understand, of the puzzle Lydia and Bessie expected to fit together; but suddenly these things mattered very little. I did not need to push them out of my mind, as I had been doing; they simply dropped into insignificance.

And in the meantime I was with my family for a week. The house fell silent; but the quiet here was simpler than the kind of quiet I had lived in for the last six months. I stared at shadows that moved only with the moon, and my ears strained after echoes that weren't there. I crept downstairs again and went out to the stable, where I found Greatheart flirting delicately with the new mare, who wasn't quite ignoring him. "I'm not sure a foal next summer is on the schedule," I told him. He rubbed his head against me. "But you're not listening," I added. I took his bridle down from its hook and he raised his head at once and watched me intently. I freed the red rose that hung from the strap across the forehead, and replaced the bridle, and the horse relaxed. "Good night, little one," I said, slapping his massive hindquarters, and made my way softly back to the house. I took a deep bowl from the kitchen, filled it with water, and tiptoed back upstairs. I put rose and bowl on the window sill; and suddenly I realized that I was exhausted. I pulled my clothes off, and fell asleep as soon as I lay down.

5

Two days passed as quickly as a sigh. On the third day Greatheart and Cider were discovered to have escaped the stable, and were grazing, side by side, by the enchanted stream. Greatheart, to everyone's surprise, was inclined to get a little huffy and snorty when Ger went to catch him, and wouldn't let him near the mare, who stood still, ears forward, and awaited developments. I had been watching the show from the kitchen door, chewing lazily on a piece of bread and Grace's blackberry jelly, but then I went across to join them. "Your overgrown lapdog has some temperament after all," said Ger with a rueful smile.

"I'll try," I said. "We could be all day chasing them.

"Here, you great idiot," I continued, walking towards the horse, who stood in front of his mare, watching my approach, "you've had your fun, a proper night of it I daresay. Now you can behave. Duty calls." I stopped a few feet away, and held my hand out, palm up, with the last of the bread and jelly. "I'll put you in with the cow if you're not good," I added. We held each other's eyes for a moment, then Greatheart dropped his head with a sigh, and ambled over to me, and put his nose in my hand. "Cart-horse," I said affectionately, and slid the halter I had thoughtfully brought with me over his head. Greatheart only flicked an ear as Ger slid a rope around the docile Cider's neck, and we returned them to the stable, Greatheart investigating all my pockets for more bread. "This should be quite a foal," said Ger. "I hope it takes after its daddy."

"Maybe she'll follow the family precedent and have twins," I suggested. The father of the twins gave me a pained look, and we went in to breakfast.

I still hadn't told Grace about Robbie; I dreaded it, knowing the heartache she had already been through, and while I knew that what I had seen in the Beast's glass was true, it was so little, so very little to ruin Grace's precarious peace of mind. And since the Beast was *persona non grata* at home anyway, I disliked the prospect of explaining the source of my information; my family would not have the faith I did in his veracity, and the possibility of truth in what I had seen would cause an uproar in several different directions at once. So I continued to put it off, and continued to scold myself feebly for so doing.

But that afternoon the minister came to call. Hope and Grace and I were all in the kitchen, and Grace asked us with a look to stay. I had not seen Pat Lawrey since my return, and I found myself estimating his worth with the cold calculation Ger used on a fresh load of pig iron, as he smiled and shook my hand and told me how well I was looking and how glad everyone was to see me. He was a nice young man, to be sure, I thought, but not much else. Grace can't marry him, I thought with a touch of fear; no wonder she still remembers Robbie. Tonight, I thought. No more delays.

Melinda's son John, the boy who worked for Ger, had spread the word of my return the day after my unexpected arrival, and the house since then had seen a steady stream of visitors, some of them old friends like Melinda and her large family, and some merely acquaintances curious to see the prodigal. All wanted to know what life in the city was like, and I put most of their questions off, and lied uncomfortably when I had to. Everyone thought it was very odd that I had turned up so suddenly, like a mushroom, or a changeling in a cradle.

Melinda had come the very first day; John had gone home for his dinner at noon, instead of eating with us, so he could start broadcasting the news as soon as possible. Melinda came back with him in the afternoon, and kissed me and shook me by the shoulders and told me I looked marvelous and how I'd grown! Her questions were the hardest to turn aside; she wanted very much to know why she hadn't seen me coming through town—everything that happened in Blue Hill happened in front of the Griffin—and what my aunt meant by letting me come alone, and whether there really had been no warning.

She obviously thought I was being treated very shabbily, and only her good manners prevented her from saying so outright. I tried to explain that I'd left the party I traveled with for only the last few miles, but she refused to be mollified. Then she was shocked that I could stay only a week—"After six, seven months, and a six weeks' journey to come here at all? The woman's mad. When are you coming again?"

"I don't know," I said unhappily.

"You don't—" she started, saw the expression on my face, and stopped abruptly. "Well, I'll say no more. These are family matters, and I've no call to be meddling. There's more here than you care to tell me, and that's as it should be; I'm no kin of yours. But I'm fond of you, child, so I hope you'll excuse me; I'd have liked to have seen more of you, but you're here for so little I'll have to leave you to your family."

I was glad to see her, but her common sense and my inability to answer her straightforward questions distressed me, and I was relieved when she took her leave. The only bright spot was watching her and Father together: They spoke for a few minutes apart from the rest of us, after she had already bid us good-bye. They were smiling at each other in a foolish sort of way that they obviously weren't aware of; and I caught Hope watching them narrowly. She caught my eye, smiled just enough for me to recognize it as a smile; and winked slowly. We turned our backs on them and returned to the kitchen, where Grace had gone already, soberly discussing the dyeing of yarn.

John also took home the tale of the wonderful new bellows—brass-bound!—that I had brought from the city, which served to soften the opinions of people like his mother toward my evil-minded aunt. Ger had found the bellows hung mysteriously in the place of the old ones, which had disappeared, a scant few minutes before John had arrived that first morning after I had come home, and had just the presence of mind to explain where they were from. John swore they were more than twice as easy to pump as the old ones, for all they were so much bigger.

The smooth white road that had brought me to my own back door had disappeared as though it had never been. That morning, while Ger was discovering his new equipment, I was walking along the edge of the forest. I could find Greatheart's hoofprints, where he had jumped over the thorny hedge that grew irregularly at the forest's border, but behind it, nothing. Nothing but rocks and leaves and dirt and pine needles: no road, no hoofprints, no sign even of any large animal forcing its way through the underbrush.

I was still staring at Greatheart's hoofprints as though they were runes when the first visitors arrived with work for Ger and Father, and discovered the lost lamb returned to the fold. The house was full of people for that day, and the day after, and the day after; I'd forgotten there were so many people in Blue Hill. But my mysterious arrival piqued their curiosity, and many of the men still remembered Greatheart's strength, and came out to wish us well, and to drink some of our cider.

That third day, Molly arrived shortly before Mr. Lawrey left, ostensibly to deliver a big jar of Melinda's famous pickles, which she remembered I was fond of, but actually to ask me again about the city. "She must keep you locked in the *attic*," Molly said impulsively. "You haven't seen *anything*."

"Well, mostly I study," I said apologetically.

Molly shook her head in wonder; and then some men who had come to consult with Father and Ger were brought in for tea. It wasn't till after dinner that evening, the dishes washed and the candles lit, that we were alone, and had time to talk. I had been seeing Robbie in my mind all afternoon, since the minister had left: his thin face lit up by the old happy-go-lucky smile I remembered from the city, when he was making the final preparations for the journey that would make him a fortune and win him a wife.

We were sitting around the parlour fire, busy with handwork, just as I remembered from the days before Father's fateful journey. I was mending harness; everyone had protested against my working, when I was only a few days home, but I had insisted; and it felt good to be doing this homely work again, although my fingers were slower than they once had been. Everything seemed very much as I remembered it: I derived much comfort from looking around me and reiterating this to myself. I wanted to take as much of this contentment and security back with me as I could.

Hope finished a seam on the dress she was making, and dragged me away from my bits of leather to use me as a dressmaker's dummy, pinning folds of green cotton around me. "This isn't going to help you much," I said, holding my arms out awkwardly as she pinned a swath across my chest. "I'm the wrong shape." Hope smiled, and spoke through a mouthful of pins. "No you're not," she said. "All I have to do is shorten the hem. Aren't there any mirrors in that grand castle of yours? I don't understand how you could help noticing something. . . ."

"She's never noticed anything but books and horses since she was a baby," said Grace, golden head bowed over a shirt she was making for Richard.

"An ugly baby," I said.

"Let's not start that again," said Hope. "Don't fidget, I'll be finished sooner, you silly thing, if you'll stand still."

"The pins stick me," I complained.

"They wouldn't, if you would stand still," Hope said

inexorably. "But didn't you grow out of your clothes, and have to have new ones?"

"Well, no," I said. "Lydia and Bessie always tend to my wardrobe, and one way or another whatever they put on me fits."

"Whew," said Hope. "I wish the twins' clothes would do that."

"Mmm," said Grace, biting off a thread.

"But that even you shouldn't notice *anything*," said Hope, kneeling to fold up the hem.

"Well—the day after I came home I looked at Greatheart's saddle," I offered, trying to be helpful. "I remember that the stirrup leathers were replaced the first day I was there. I'm using them three holes longer now than I did then. Funny though, I don't at all remember moving them."

"What did I tell you?" said Grace, starting on another seam. "Only Beauty would think to measure herself by the length of her stirrups," and everybody laughed. "Oh dear," said Hope. "I've lost a pin. Richard's foot will find it tomorrow. All right, foolish girl, you can take it off now."

"How?" I said plaintively.

After I had been extricated I sat down on the edge of the stone hearth, where I had set my cup of cider, near

Grace's knee. I hated to break the comfortable silence. "I—there's another reason I came home, just now," I said; and everyone stopped whatever they were doing and looked at me. The silence was splintered, not just by my words. I looked down into my cup. "I've been putting off telling you. It's—it's about Grace."

My oldest sister laid the little shirt on her knees and crossed her hands over it before she looked at me; and then her eyes were anxious. "What is it?"

I didn't know any good way to lead up to it. "Robbie's come home," I said, very low. "He put in at the city dock the morning of the day I came home. I came to tell you—so you wouldn't marry Mr. Lawrey till you'd seen him again."

Grace gasped when I first mentioned Robbie's name, and put out her hands, which I seized. "Robbie?" she said. "Oh, is it true? I can't believe it, I've thought of it for so long. Beauty, is it true?"

I nodded as she stared at me, and then her eyes went blank, and she fell forwards in my lap in a faint. I lifted her gently back into her chair as the rest of the family stood up and started forwards. Father slid a pillow under her head, and Hope disappeared into the kitchen and returned with an evil-smelling little bottle. Grace stirred and sat up, looking at us as we crouched around her. "It had better be true, now," said Father grimly. "I know," I answered in an undertone. "But it is."

Grace looked around slowly until her eyes rested on me, and her gaze cleared. "How do you know? Tell me everything. Have you seen him? But you said he was in the city. Please—"

"I saw him the same way I saw you and Hope talking in the parlour, that morning," I said, and her eyes widened, and I heard Hope catch her breath. "The *White Raven* is a wreck; I don't know how he managed to bring her home at all. And he looks ill, and tired. But he's alive. And I don't know what he'll do when he finds out what's happened to you—to all of us."

"Alive," whispered Grace, and she looked at Father, with her eyes as big and bright as summer raindrops. "We must invite him to come here as soon as he may. He can rest here, and regain his strength."

Father stood up and walked around the room, and paused as he returned to the fireplace. "You're sure," he said to me, wishing for reassurance and yet unsure that he could accept it. I nodded.

"Magic," murmured Ger. "Ah, well."

Father took another turn around the room—it was

too small a room for a man of his size and hasty stride—and paused again. "I shall write to him at once. There will be business arrangements to be made also. Perhaps I should go myself." He stood irresolute.

"No need," said Ger. "Callaway is setting out for the city in a few days' time. He asked me today if there was anything he could do for us—offered to escort Beauty, too, since her aunt doesn't seem to be providing for her properly. You can trust him with any messages. If you tell him to bring Tucker back with him, you may be sure he will, tied on the back of his saddle if need be."

Father smiled. "Yes, Nick Callaway is a good man. I'd rather not make that journey again if I can." Everyone avoided looking in my direction. After a tiny pause, Father turned to Grace. "My dear, six years is a long time. Perhaps you should wait and see?"

"Wait?" she said. "I've been waiting six years. Robbie won't have forgotten, any more than I have. And we're on even terms now, too; neither of us has a penny of our own." This was not strictly true; by Blue Hill's standards, we were very well off. But Grace swept us all before her on the bright, happy look she wore, which we had not seen on her face for six years. "It will be all right," she said. "I will not wait any longer."

Ger and Hope exchanged glances and slow smiles.

"Send for him, Father," said Grace; her tone was that of a queen commanding, with no thought of delay or denial. "Please. I will write to him also."

"Very well," said Father.

The next three days crept past me as quickly and secretly as the first three had; perhaps even faster, because after my news of Robbie, we were all preoccupied with him and with Grace, who could scarcely remember to put one foot in front of the other when she walked; with the sudden, brutal urgency of a long and terrible wait ended. Her letter and Father's were delivered to Nick Callaway, who after being assured that I needed no escort declared his intention of setting off on the very next day. "I've no reason to hang about, and I'm anxious to get back before the weather turns—it's risky enough, as late in the year as it is," he said. "I should be there in five weeks, if I'm lucky, and home again in twelve, with your friend, I hope." He obviously thought there was something a little odd in my arrangements, but he inquired no further after I had reassured him that I was well taken care of. "But my party will be traveling much more slowly than you," I said.

"All right, miss, and a good journey to you," he said,

and rode away, leaving us to be grateful that he hadn't asked us where our mysterious information about Captain Tucker's whereabouts had come from in the first place.

On the sixth night I said, "I will have to leave tomorrow, you know"; and everyone spoke at once, begging me to stay one more day. I sat on the fender, twisting my ring around my finger, listening unhappily. Hope and Grace both started crying. I said nothing for several minutes, and the tumult subsided at last, and everyone was silent, like mourners at graveside. Father stood up and put his hand on my shoulder. "One more day," he said. "It's not even been a full week yet."

I chewed my lip, felt the whole weight of my family's love concentrated in my father's hand, pushing me down where I sat. "All right," I said with difficulty.

I slept badly that night. My sleep had been dreamless, these days at home; in the mornings I had felt vaguely cheated, but had each day quickly forgotten it in the pleasure of being able to go downstairs and see my father and sisters, brother, and niece and nephew over the breakfast table. But this night I dreamed in haunted snatches of the castle, of vast empty rooms, of the sinister silence I had feared during my first days there.

But now it was worse, because my sixth sense caused it to echo through my mind till my own body felt like a shell, a cold stony cavern with nothing in it but the wind. The comforting if ambiguous presence I had learned to trust during the last few months had disappeared; the castle was as solitary and incalcuable as it had been on my first night there. Where was my Beast? I could not find him, nor could I sense him anywhere.

I woke up at dawn, rumpled and unrefreshed, and stared at the low slanted ceiling for several minutes before I could get myself out of bed. I was moody and distracted all that day, and nothing pleased me; I did not belong here, and I should not stay. I tried to hide my impatience, but my family watched me unhappily, and uncomprehendingly, till I could not meet anyone's eyes. That evening as I huddled by the fire, my hands idle but restless, Father said: "You will leave tomorrow morning?" His voice was a little unsteady.

I looked up at him, around at all of them. "I *must*. I'm sorry. Please try to understand. I promised."

Father tried to smile, but didn't quite manage it. "You were well named," he said. "At least—I will still dream about you often?"

I nodded.

"At least I know that much now," he said with an effort.

I couldn't speak, and soon afterwards I went upstairs. I laid aside the plain clothes that Grace and Hope had lent me, and shook out the creases in the dress I had worn when I arrived; my sisters had wanted to wash and press it for me, but I had refused; there was no need to give them extra work. They acceded to what they were pleased to term my perversity eventually; with great practical knowledge of such matters, they said I would ruin my lovely dress, but I shook my head. I would leave it to Lydia's and Bessie's inspired care. There was little packing to do; then I lay down and tried to sleep. But this night was worse than the last, and I tossed and turned and clawed at the bed-clothes. I fell asleep at last, but my dreams were troubled.

I dreamed that I was walking through the castle, looking for the Beast, and, as in my dreams of the night before, I could not find him. "I am easily found, if you want me," he had said. But I hurried through room after room after room, and no Beast, nor any sense of his presence. At last I came to the little room where I had first found him, and where I had seen Robbie in the glass. He was sitting in the deep armchair as if he had never moved since I had left him a week before; his hands lay palm up on his knees, but the right one was curled shut.

"Oh, Beast," I said, "I thought I would never find you." But he never stirred. "Beast!" I cried. "Oh, Beast! He's dead, and it's all my fault"—and I woke up. The weak grey light that serves as harbinger of red and golden dawn faintly lit my window. I fumbled for a candle, found and lit it, and by its little light saw that the rose floating in the bowl was dying. It had already lost most of its petals, which floated on the water like tiny, unseaworthy boats, deserted for safer craft.

"Dear God," I said. "I must go back at once." I dressed and hurried downstairs, finding my way by touch through the home I no longer remembered; no one else was stirring. I left the one full saddle-bag we had never opened, and picked up the other, which was more than ample for my small needs; the bags had lain undisturbed all this week on the table in the corner of the parlour. I picked up some bread and dried meat from the kitchen and ran to the stable. I had marked the tree beside which I had found Greatheart's hoofprints the morning after my arrival, and now I led my anxious horse along the border of the forest till I recognized the white knife slash in the bark of the tree. I mounted, adjusting harness as I rode, and Greatheart was soon crashing through the brush.

But we didn't find the road. This did not disturb me at first; we jogged, trotted, and cantered steadily till the morning sun lit our way for us, and the forest floor showed a patchwork green and gold and brown. "You need only get lost in the woods," I recalled. The edge of the forest was long since out of sight. I turned to make sure; beyond trees I saw shadows of trees, and then shadows of shadows. I dismounted, loosened the girths, and fed myself and the horse some bread; then we walked on side by side for a little while, till Greatheart was cool. Then my impatience grew too great, and I remounted and we cantered on.

Trees slapped me in the face, and Greatheart's gait was uneven as he picked his way over the rough ground. It seemed to get worse the farther we went. It hadn't been like this on the other two journeys. By noon we were tired and blown, and Greatheart walked without fidgeting to go faster. My father and I had struck the road after only a few hours' easy riding. I dismounted again, and we walked together, the foam dripping out of the horse's mouth. We came at last to a little stream; we both waded and drank and splashed our hot faces with the cool water. I noticed the water had an odd taste, a little bitter, which lingered in the mouth a long time after drinking.

We turned and followed the course of the stream, for want of a better guide. The way was a little easier here; the trees and thornbushes did not grow so closely together near the water, where the ground was softer and covered with low leafy bushes and marsh grass. The stream murmured to itself, but paid us no heed, and the sharp smell of the grasses Greatheart broke underfoot bit our throats. The sun walked down the afternoon sky, and I saw no sign of the road we were looking for. I knew from glimpses of the sun through the trees that we were still heading in more or less the direction we had started from before dawn; but perhaps this was of no use in this forest. Nor did I know if the Beast's castle lay at the geographical center of the forest, nor whether we were heading towards the center at all. We could only go on. Twilight came upon us; we were lost in good earnest now. I had little notion of woodcraft. I had had no notion that it might be necessary.

Greatheart strode doggedly on. We had been traveling for over twelve hours, and even Greatheart was nearing the end of his strength; we had stopped to rest infrequently and briefly. I couldn't rest. I dismounted and we walked. Greatheart stumbled occasionally, more often as the shadows grew up around us. I didn't notice if I stumbled or not, although when I stood still to look up at the sky my feet in their soft slippers took advantage of the pause to tell me that they were sore and bruised. Greatheart stood still, his big head hanging. "This will help a little," I said, and took off his saddle and bridle, and hung them neatly on a convenient tree-limb. "Maybe we'll be able to come back for them." I took what remained of the food I had brought, then hung the saddlebag over the pommel. After a moment's thought, I pulled off my heavy skirt, added it to the pile, and tied my cloak over my petticoats and twisted it tightly around me with a ribbon. "Come along," I said. Greatheart shook himself gingerly and looked at me. "I don't know what's happening either. Come along." And he followed me. The absence of that skirt made a big difference to my feet.

The last bit of daylight was fading and leaving the silver water black when I saw something pale glimmer through the trees to my left. It was long and low, too still and too straight for running water. I caught my breath, and began to struggle through the suddenly dense undergrowth, Greatheart snorting and crashing behind me. It was the road. It stretched out to my right, and ended a few feet to my left, in ragged patches of sand and stone. It did not run as smooth and straight as I remembered, but my eyes were blurred and tired. My feet touched the road just as the last light died, leaving the road a grey smudge in the blackness.

"We'll have to wait till moonrise now," I said fretfully. After standing, looking uselessly around me for a few minutes, I went back to the side of the road and sat down under a tree. Greatheart investigated me, then wandered out into the sandy road and had a good roll, with much snorting and blowing and waving of legs. He returned to drip dust on me, and I fed him some more bread. He ate a few leaves off the tree I was under, then settled down on three legs for a nap. I sat, hands around my knees, waiting till the moon climbed high enough for us to make out our way. It seemed like hours, but it wasn't long; the moon rose early, the sky was clear and cloudless; even the starlight was bright enough to cast a few shadows through the tangled undergrowth. The road was a dim pale ribbon, leading farther into the forest, promising nothing. I sighed, then walked over to the horse and thumped his shoulder. He opened his eyes and looked at me. "Do you think you might be ridden?" I rubbed some of the dirt off his back with a corner of my cloak, and mounted with the aid of a low-hanging branch. I had first taught him to respond to my legs and voice when he was a yearling, before he had ever worn any harness; but that was a long time ago, and I felt very insecure on a back as broad as his was now, without a saddle. But he stepped onto the road and broke into a gentle trot, little more than a shuffle, and I clung to his mane and managed fairly well. I found myself falling asleep as I rode. All that kept me awake at all was the horse's changes of gait, walk to jog, a brief canter, and walk again, as he set his own pace. His head was up and his ears pricked;—I concentrated on not falling off—and on not thinking what might lie ahead of me. First we had to find the castle.

Any number of nights may have passed without my knowledge or comprehension. Greatheart shifted from a jog to a walk, and then stopped altogether. I opened my eyes and looked around vaguely. We had come to the big silver gates, but they remained closed, even when Greatheart put his nose out and touched them. I kneed the horse around till I could reach out and push them with my hand; the surface was smooth and slightly chilly to the flat of my palm. Then it quivered like the skin of an animal, and seemed to flush with a warm grey light like the earth's first dawn. It swung open slowly with the sound of someone breathing. I did not wonder at this long; Greatheart broke into a gallop as soon as the gates opened wide enough to let us through. I dug in with my hands and legs and held on.

We didn't see the castle till we were almost upon it. It was dark, darker than the shadows around it; even the moonlight shunned it. The lights in the garden were few and dim, and blocked to us as we galloped through the meadow and the stand of ornamental trees. Greatheart went straight to the stable and stopped. I slid off his back, my legs almost folding under me when my feet touched the ground. The stable door didn't open. I put both hands against it, and it shuddered, as the gate had; but it remained shut. I pushed it in the direction it usually opened, and as slowly and wearily as Sisyphus I forced it open. One or two candles lit wanly as we went in. I opened a stall door and sent Greatheart in, hot as he was, threw a blanket over him, gave him a swift pat and word of thanks, and left him. I would tend him later. I had to find the Beast.

The great front doors to the castle were open, to my intense relief. I ran inside. A lantern lit, its wick nearly guttering. I picked it up and adjusted it; it was plain hammered copper, with a glass bubble to protect the flame. I carried it with me down the corridor. The dining hall was cold and still, like the parlour opposite, though both the doors stood wide. I went upstairs.

It was much worse than my dreams had been. I was tired, deadly tired, and sore and hungry, and so filthy that the creases of my petticoats chafed me when I moved; and my feet hurt worse with every step. I was too tired to think; all that my mind held was: "I must find my Beast." But I couldn't find him. I was too tired even to call aloud to him, and too numb to hear even if he had answered. All my senses were dull; I could catch no feeling of his presence. The castle had never been so large. I crossed hundreds of halls, passed through thousands of rooms. I didn't even find my room, nor did I hear any rustling that might have been Bessie or Lydia. The castle was deserted, and as chill and dank as if it had stood empty for many years. Some of the thicker shadows might have been dust and cobwebs. It was fortunate that I carried a lamp with me, because few of the candles lit at my approach, and many of them winked once or twice and went out again as if the effort were too much. My arm ached with holding my lantern aloft, and its light trembled with my arm's shivering; its faint glow spilled around me, but none of the shadows held the Beast. My stumbling footsteps echoed in solitude.

More time passed. I tripped over the edge of a carpet and fell sprawling; the lamp turned over and went out. I lay where I was, too exhausted to move, and found myself weeping. I dragged myself to a sitting position, disgusted at my weakness, and looked hopelessly down the long hall in the direction I had been going when I fell; and in the darkness I saw a tiny puddle of light. A light. I got to my feet and went towards it.

It was the room I had found the Beast in on the first night, and the room I had dreamed about last night. A dying fire in the hearth cast the dim light I had seen through the partly open door; it creaked on its hinges when I pushed it farther open. He was sitting in the wing chair, his closed right hand on his knee, as if he hadn't moved since I had left him over a week ago. "Beast!" I cried, and he didn't move. "You can't die. Please don't die. Come back to me," I said, weeping again, kneeling down by the chair. He didn't move. I looked around wildly. The bowl of roses still sat by his elbow. The flowers were brown, and petals lay scattered on the floor. I pulled the white handkerchief from his breast pocket and dipped it in the water, then laid it across the Beast's forehead. "My love, wake up," I said.

With a motion as slow as centuries he opened his eyes.

I didn't dare move. He blinked, and some light returned to his dull eyes, and he saw me. "Beauty," he said.

"I'm here, dear Beast," I said.

"I thought you had broken your promise," he said; there wasn't a shade of reproach in his voice, and for a moment I couldn't answer. "I started late," I said, "and then it took me a very long time to find my way through the forest."

"Yes, it would," he said, speaking with pauses between the words. "I'm sorry. I couldn't help you."

"It doesn't matter," I said, "as long as you're all right. But will you be all right now? I'll never leave you again."

He smiled. "I'll be all right. Thank you, Beauty."

I sighed, and started to get to my feet; but I staggered, and saved myself only by clutching the arm of the chair. The world splashed around me like black water in a bilge, and I couldn't find my feet. The Beast reached out a hand, and I sank onto his lap. "I'm sorry," I said.

"You're very tired, you must rest now," he said. "You're safe home."

I shook my head. Now that my most pressing fear had been disposed of, a few thoughts stole tentatively back inside my mind. "Not yet. I have to see to Greatheart— I'd still be in the forest without him—but I had to find you first—and then there's something I must tell you."

"Not now," he said.

"Yes, now," I replied. I paused a minute while the world stopped pitching and rolling. I could hear the Beast breathing; I didn't think he had been when I first entered the room. "Look," I said. "Dawn." Tendrils of pink were climbing above the forest, and a little hesitating light came through the window, and we could see each other's faces clearly. The Beast was wearing golden velvet, I noticed, instead of the dark brown I had last seen.

"I can't sleep now," I said. "It's daylight. What I want is breakfast." And I stood up, and walked to the window. As the light increased, a little of my strength returned. I leaned my elbows on the window sill and looked out across the gardens. They had never looked so beautiful to me before. The Beast joined me at the window. "It's good to be back," I said.

"Were your family pleased with the news you brought?" he said.

I nodded. "Yes. Grace won't be good for anything now, till they have had proper news of him. But that's all right too. They hope he'll ride back with the man who's carrying her and Father's letters to him. Will you let me—sometimes—look in the glass again?" I added timidly.

The Beast nodded. "Of course. You know, though, I feel a little sorry for the young minister."

I looked out the window again. I waved a hand, indicating vaguely the sweep of garden and meadow, and said, "You—this hasn't suffered any lasting harm by my—er—delay, has it?"

"No, Beauty, don't worry," he said.

I hesitated. "What would have happened—if I hadn't come?"

"Happened? Nothing," he said. "Nothing at all."

I stared at him, not comprehending, as his answer hung between us in the morning air. "Nothing? But—" And I stopped, not wanting to mention, or remember, his dreadful stillness when I had first entered the room.

"I was dying?" he said. "Yes. I would have died, and you and Greatheart would have returned to your family; and in another two hundred years this castle would have been lost in a garden run wild, with the forest growing up to the dooryard, and birds nesting in the towers. And in two hundred years after that, even the legends would have left, and only the stones remained."

I took a deep breath. "This is what I have to tell you then," I said, looking up at him. The Beast looked at me inquiringly. I looked down again, and said in a rush, to the grey stones of the window sill, "I love you, and I want to marry you." Perhaps I fainted, but it wasn't at all like the first time. The Beast disappeared, and then everything else did too, or perhaps it all happened at once. There was a wild explosion of light, as if the sun had burst; then, like a shock wave, there rose up a great din of what sounded like bells ringing, huge cathedral bells, and crowds shouting and cheering, horses neighing, even cannons firing. I huddled down where I stood and pressed my hands to my ears, but this helped not at all. The castle trembled underfoot as if the stones were applauding in their foundations; and then I could feel nothing under my feet at all, and I was buoyed up by light and sound. Then it all ceased as quickly as it had begun. I lowered my hands and opened my eyes cautiously. The gardens looked just the same; perhaps the sunlight was a bit brighter; but then it was morning, and the sun was rising. I turned around and looked into the room.

The Beast was nowhere to be seen. A man stood beside me, dressed in golden velvet, as the Beast had been, with white lace at his throat and wrists. He had brown eyes, and curly brown hair streaked with grey. He was taller than I was, though not so tall as the Beast; and as I looked at him in surprise, he smiled at me, a little uncertainly it seemed.

He was quite alarmingly handsome, and I blinked and felt foolish. "My Beast," I said, and my voice sounded shrill. I felt like a scrubby schoolgirl beside this grand gentleman. "Where is he? I must go find him—" And I backed away from the window, still looking at my unexpected visitor.

"Wait, Beauty," the man said.

I stopped. "Your voice," I said. "I know your voice."

"I am the Beast," he said. "I was laid under an enchantment to live as a dreadful Beast until some maiden should love me in spite of my ugliness, and promise to marry me."

I continued to stare bemusedly at him. My voice sounded weak and silly in my ears: "Your voice—I recognize it, but it sounds different." I said inanely: "Is it really you? I mean—I—well, I find this rather—er—difficult. . . ." I trailed off, and put my hands to my face, pinching my chin as if reassuring myself that I was awake; and heard the clink of bracelets falling back from my wrists.

"Yes, I am really I," he said gently; "but my voice is coming from a smaller—human—chest now."

"You're the young man in the last picture," I said suddenly.

He smiled wryly. "Yes; but not so young now, I'm

afraid. Even enchantments aren't perfect protection against time. But then I don't feel like a young man anymore." He looked down at his hands. "It took me the first decade just to learn to walk like a man again."

"Who did this to you?" I said, and backed up against the window ledge, grateful for its support, as I had been grateful for the support of a balustrade on another first meeting months ago.

He frowned. "It's an old family curse of sorts. My forebears were, um, rather overpious, and overzealous in impressing their neighbors with their piety. After the first few generations of holier-than-thou the local magician got rather tired of them, and cursed them; but unfortunately their virtue was even as great as they made it out to be, and the curse wouldn't stick. So, being a magician, he settled down to wait for their first erring step. My family laughed, which didn't improve his temper any—and unfortunately for me, at last, that erring foot was mine.

"You've probably noticed the carving around the front doors." I nodded. "That was I, two centuries ago." He looked away, and when he looked back at me, his smile was strained. "I'm sorry I'm so old—I think it works out to about one year in ten—I've been waiting a long time.

I can't let you off now, you know. I hope you don't mind very much."

"I can't marry *you*," I burst out, and the smile left his face as if it had been cut off, and his eyes were dark and sad. I blundered on: "Look at you. You should marry a queen or something, a duchess at least, not a dull drab little nothing like myself. I haven't anything—no dowry, not even a title to hide behind."

"Beauty—" he began.

"And you needn't consider yourself in my debt because I've undone your enchantment for you. You've"—I rushed on—"done a great deal for—for my family, and for me. I'll never forget—my months here."

His expression had become quizzical as I was speaking. "Let's leave aside my debt, ah, or responsibility for the moment. As I recall, we had a conversation along similar lines at the beginning of our acquaintance. You suffer from the oddest misapprehensions about your appearance." He looked over his shoulder. "If I remember correctly, there should be a mirror that has reappeared just outside, in the hall. Come." He held out his hand, and I reluctantly put mine in his, and heard the clink of bracelets again, and looked down. "Good heavens!" I exclaimed. "They've done it *again*. How—?"

I was wearing the silver princess's dress; the skirts drifted around me in a shining mist, and I wondered how I hadn't noticed before that my straggling hair was clean again, and combed, and pinned to my head. I seemed to have had a bath while the foundations had danced under me, and my exhaustion had been washed away with the grime of travel. I felt the griffin necklace around my throat, and the high-heeled shoes on my feet.

I tried to pull my hand free when I noticed the change, but his fingers closed around mine. "Come," he repeated. I didn't have much choice. I followed him unhappily out into the hall, and there, as he had said, was a mirror in a golden frame, big enough to hold a reflection of both of us as we stood side by side and looked into it.

The girl in the mirror wasn't I, I was sure of it, in spite of the fact that the man in golden velvet was holding my hand as he was holding the girl's. She was tall—well, all right, I said to myself, I do remember that I'm tall enough now. Her hair was a pale coppery red, and her eyes, strangest of all, weren't muddy hazel, but clear and amber, with flecks of green. And the dress did look lovely on her, in spite of the fact that she was blushing furiously—I felt as if I were blushing furiously too. I leaned closer, fascinated. No, there, it *was* I, after all: The quirk of the eyebrows was still there, the dark uneven arch that had always said that the eyes didn't believe what they saw; but then since I had only seen them in mirrors, perhaps this was true. And I recognized the high wide cheekbones, but my face had filled out around them; and the mouth was still higher on one side than the other, and the high side had a dimple.

"Are you convinced?" said the man in the mirror.

"Oh dear," said the girl. "It's magic, it'll fade away. It's not possible."

He put his hands on my bare shoulders and turned me to face him. "I should warn you, my darling, that we haven't much time. Things all over the castle will be waking up, and discovering they exist again, and then coming to find me, and to meet their new mistress. There's no magic left that can hurt you, nor any that remains that will fade away. Your family will be arriving soon—with Robbie— and if our minister wakes up in time and remembers where he left his Bible, we can have the wedding this afternoon. Double, if you like, with your sister."

I had a brief vision of my family riding over the meadows towards the castle. Behind them I noticed that the holly hedge was gone; the silver gates framed a broad white road that led through a park that had once been a dark enchanted forest. Hope rode the chestnut mare, Cider; Grace rode a horse only a few shades paler than her glorious hair. Ger's and Robbie's mounts were blood bays, with black legs and ears; brown Odysseus carried Father, and Melinda rode beside him on a cream-colored mare, her rose-silk skirts falling like water over the mare's white shoulders, her face as bright as my sisters'. My family was dressed in the rich things I had found in my saddle-bag: Father in white and the iridescent blue of aquamarines, Ger in red and grey and black, as fine as a lord, riding beside Hope in her green dress and sea-colored emeralds. Grace was next, in gold brocade and rubies, and Robbie, in scarlet and green, rode close beside her, holding her hand, healthy and strong and happy again. I could still see the white in his hair, but now the vivid contrast suited him, lending his handsome face a wisdom and dignity beyond his years.

Behind them hundreds of people walked the white road; more road in carriages, and on horseback, splendid as the procession for a king's coronation. The last of them were so far away that I could not distinguish them from the green leaves and the flowers, and the singing birds.

Then the image faded as the man who stood beside me continued: "I love you, Beauty. Will you marry me?"

"Yes," I said, and he took me in his golden arms, and kissed me. When we parted, it was only to a hand's length, and we looked long at one another, smiling.

He raised my hand to his lips, held it there for a moment. "Shall we go down now?" he said.

I turned my head, listening to a purposeful stirring in the castle halls beneath us. Little tremors of sound and motion licked the threshold of the pilastered hall we stood in alone; but I thought my ear picked out an individual rustling it knew well. "I think I hear Lydia."

He turned his head also. "Very likely. I'm afraid you'll find there are a good many Lydias about the castle now. I can recall a veritable army of housekeepers, each more enthusiastic than the last." He paused. "You know about Lydia and Bessie, then?"

I nodded. "I've been listening—rather a captive audience, you know—to their conversations for several months now. Since the night I fainted," I said shyly. "You know. When I began to learn to see."

He smiled. "Yes, I know." More briskly he added: "Then you're a little prepared. They've been very good to me; they needn't have stayed when the change came, but they chose to, for my sake—for the sake of what remained of my humanity. Although I can admit now that sometimes their common-sense attitude towards everything, including being enchanted, could be as much an irritation as a comfort. I daresay you know something of that."

"Yes, I do," I said, and dropped my eyes from his a moment. "I worried often about what it was I had to figure out, and about the last hope they couldn't talk about."

"You understand now, don't you?" he said, and raised my chin again with his finger. "The terms of the magic were that you agree to marry the Beast. Not something that Bessie and Lydia, with their silver-polish and dust-under-the-rug consciences, could understand. I'm sorry."

I smiled. "I understand now. But it doesn't matter and you needn't apologize. They have been very kind to me too. Even if we did differ a little about suitable dresses."

He considered me a moment, a mischievous light creeping into his eyes, and said: "Was *that* the dress—that night you wouldn't come out of your room?"

I grinned and nodded, and we both laughed; and the last shadows fled away from the corners of the castle and flew out of the window like bats, never to return.

He drew my hand through his arm; far below us in the bright, sunlit courtyard we heard a clatter of hoofs, and

Grace's laugh as she dismounted. Then I heard Melinda's voice, and Father's answering her. "A triple ceremony, I think?" said my lover.

Ger said: "Where Greatheart is, Beauty cannot be far away."

I saw my horse standing, tall and proud and shining like the sky before a storm in winter, his mane riding his crest like thunderheads on the horizon. He was draped in crimson and gold, and a red rose was tucked under the crownpiece of his bridle. Beside him a black horse stood, like him enough that the two could have been brothers; his saddle was silver, and the trailing skirts sapphire blue; and a white rose gleamed like the moon between his black ears. Just as I saw the two grooms, dressed in green and white, standing at the horses' heads, and several more assisting my family—and then more, striding out of the stable doors, dressed in their livery, with red and white roses at their breasts, going to assist the crowd of people collecting in the courtyard—the image faded once again.

I turned back to the man at my side. "I don't even know your name."

He smiled. "I'm afraid I no longer remember it. You will have to name me. Come; introduce me to your family. I am looking forward to meeting them."

"I am looking forward to their meeting you," I said, and we left the hall that held the room where Beauty first met the Beast, and descended the stairs together, as thousands of candles in the crystal chandeliers blazed in greeting, till they rivaled the light of the sun. As we approached the great front hall, the doors swung open, and the sea of sound and scent and color swept in and foamed around our feet. My family stood nearest the threshold, and they looked up with glad expectancy. The crowd caught sight of us, and everyone sent up a cheer; Greatheart and his brother neighed and stamped, and above it all rang the wild music of bells and pipes and horns.